DOWN A DARK ALLEY

by Genevieve Holden

DOWN A DARK ALLEY
DON'T GO IN ALONE
DEADLIER THAN THE MALE
SOMETHING'S HAPPENED TO KATE
THE VELVET TARGET
SOUND AN ALARM
KILLER LOOSE!

DOWN A DARK ALLEY

GENEVIEVE HOLDEN

PUBLISHED FOR THE CRIME CLUB BY
DOUBLEDAY & COMPANY, INC.
GARDEN CITY, NEW YORK
1976

All of the characters in this book are fictitious, and any resemblance to actual persons, living or dead, is purely coincidental.

Library of Congress Cataloging in Publication Data

Pou, Genevieve Long, 1919–
    Down a dark alley.

    I. Title.
PZ4.P782Dt [PS3566.O75]   813'.5'4
ISBN 0-385-11188-6
Library of Congress Catalog Card Number 75-20748
Copyright © 1976 by Genevieve Holden Pou
All Rights Reserved
Printed in the United States of America
First Edition

For the
Midtown Neighborhood Association

Chapter One

Atlanta was basking in a luminous excess of October's bright blue weather. The sun shone with majestic impartiality on mansions and hovels, cottages and condominiums. The air that day was rated "acceptable." This acceptably polluted air was the temperature recommended for table wines. Birds twittered and hopped madly about amid the burnished splendor of scarlet, copper, and gold leaves.

It was altogether a corker of a day, the sort of day newspaper horoscopes foresee as "propitious for beginning new projects."

On Mimosa Way, projects for the day were apt to be simple and basic or complex and sophisticated, depending on the type of dwelling in which they were being planned. For Mimosa Way was in Midtown and typical of the section's richly varied social strata. Midtown was an old section that had started out respectable, deteriorated into raffishness, and had now reached a point in its resurgence where its future prosperity, if not absolutely assured, was at least dimly discernible.

Thus, the fine weather offered a little colony of winos, who lived in an old ruin, a chance to earn some drinking money by raking leaves and sweeping driveways. And in a walled villa next door, a young professor and his wife debated on whether to go to a meeting of an encounter group that had been marred by a middle-aged banker who regarded the massage sessions as opportunities for anatomical exploration of the female members. In one house on Mimosa Way, murder was the project under consideration. It was being taken out of the category labeled "unthinkable" and contemplated as a handy solution to a knotty problem.

Farther down the street in a restored Edwardian house, Dinah Prentiss mulled over the meeting she was to attend that night.

She gazed out the kitchen window at a riot of color reminiscent of Matisse on his bolder days. Orange and yellow and red leaves formed a filagreed frame for orange and green plastic garbage cans in the back yard next door.

She was in that languid state of contentment brought on by a lovely Saturday preceded by a satisfactory week. A Saturday with pleasant evening prospects and nothing jarring in between. Or at least nothing scheduled. She never discounted the possibility of the non-scheduled disaster.

The gas flames sent a pot of coffee into a fit of fiendish chuckling and speckled with tan and gold a sputtering slice of french toast.

Dinah poured a cup of coffee and took her plate across the room to a marble-topped Empire table for what should be, by all reasonable expectations, a late, leisurely breakfast, a suitably sybaritic reward for someone who has worked her ass off all week at an exacting job.

Dinah was an editorial assistant on a prestigious and highly unprofitable magazine called *The Southern Conservationist*. Profit, however, was not necessary for its survival. It was owned and financed by Martin Sterling, a notoriously eccentric multi-millionaire who, having laid waste to vast tracts of woodland with a multitude of hideous subdivisions, was now expiating his guilt by attacking pollution and decimation of wildlife.

She picked up a syrup pitcher and watched the slow motion descent of a trickle of honey onto the french toast.

She had slept until 11:30, and the rest of the attenuated day would be spent on such unexacting chores as washing a few clothes and shopping at the supermarket.

In the evening she and most of the other members would gather at Custer's Last Stand, the neighborhood bar, for a meeting of the Pseudo-Intellectual Society of the South (P.I.S.S.). Membership was made up largely of those who worked at the writing profession, some rather tenuously in the backwaters of advertising and P.R., and some in the mainstreams of newspaper reporting and freelance writing of all sorts of books.

The society was not run by Robert's Rules of Order, or any other sort of order. Officers were elected by secret ballot and secret count, the secret counter being Tom Cauldon, a reporter in the local *Newsweek* bureau. He announced the election results at whatever time and place he chose.

His last announcement had been made at a regrettable time and place: a gigantic Chamber of Commerce banquet, at which the new president of P.I.S.S. had sat across the table from him. He leaned forward to shout above the din, which, unbeknownst to him, was being quelled by the emcee banging on his water glass with a knife. Cauldon, who had been chosen secret ballot counter mainly because of his lewd Malapropic plays on words, bellowed into the sudden silence, "Congratulations on your erection. You are the new President of P.I.S.S."

Meetings were held on Saturday night—any Saturday night when as many as ten or twelve members were in town with no other plans for the evening. So the society might meet for two consecutive Saturdays and not meet again for a couple of months.

The society was meeting tonight to pick the winner of the autumnal quarter's Able and Noble Teacher Award (P.I.S.S.A.N.T.). This uncoveted award was bestowed on some locally or nationally prominent person who had made the most abysmal public statement of the quarter.

Selections were made by what was called a revolving committee, the name deriving from the fact that the committee sat on the revolving stools at the bar while deliberating on their choices.

Although it would be difficult to imagine a less likely atmosphere for romance, this particular meeting was to be attended by David Winthrop, president of Winthrop Realty and new owner of Custer's Last Stand.

David was by no means a new person in Dinah's life. He was the nephew of Ted Winthrop, her grandmother's old friend and business partner. Dinah had known him for ten years. It was a divorce last year that had changed his status from invisibility to eligibility.

Dinah had gone out with him several times, and their relationship had progressed to that anticipatory stage of attraction and acute awareness which might or might not lead to the euphoric lunacy of "being in love." He had asked her out tonight, and she had invited him to sit with her at the meeting.

Later, Dinah was to tell several people that the telephone's ringing had an ominous sound, but she was claiming the ex post facto prescience almost irresistible to clairvoyants and non-seers alike.

Actually, she drifted out into the hall, still bemused with contentment, and languidly answered the phone. The premonition that all was not well did not come until an operatorish voice announced that Western Union had a telegram for Mrs. Amanda Prentiss. Dinah said that her grandmother wasn't at home, but she'd take the message.

The impersonal voice said, "Clifford and I arriving Saturday afternoon. Love, Charlotte."

Dinah stood, speechless and immobile, while the voice, with a hint of petulance, repeated, "Would you like me to read it again?"

"Oh, yes, please. I'd like to write it down." The message, which she scribbled on a memo pad, did not improve with repetition.

Recovering from the immobile stage of shock, she went into a manic phase—dashing to her room, pulling off pajamas, grabbing slacks and shirt from the closet, and running a comb through her hair. She saw in the mirror the familiar reflection of a slender girl with long, shining chestnut hair and jade-green eyes who was often described as "striking" but never as "pretty."

What on earth had possessed Aunt Charlotte to descend on them so suddenly with so little warning? Five years ago she had diagnosed her arthritis as too crippling for her to travel again. Since then she had remained safely in her home town in South Carolina, confining the menacing aspects of her personality to her own neighborhood.

Typically, she hadn't said what time. It could be any hour of the afternoon, including right now.

Dinah ran through the central hall and out the front door, pausing at the edge of the big front porch to get her breath before she descended the two flights of steps to the sidewalk.

Mimosa Way presented its usual panorama of Neapolitan hurly-burly. Bearded young men and ancient pensioners strode or tottered along the sidewalk across the street, on their way to or from the little shopping center—a bar, grocery store, launderette, and beauty shop all housed in an ancient brick building.

Behind a plastic profusion of pink hydrangeas in the window of Ethel's Beauty Salon, two wizened patrons sat like helmeted astronauts under a couple of dryers.

In the launderette next door, in the row of chairs for washing and waiting patrons, a long-haired youth reading a textbook appeared to be oblivious to all going on around him. A girl in faded shirt and jeans was manicuring her nails, probably in preparation for the emergence of evening butterfly from daytime chrysalis.

A fat housewife in tight slacks and pink rollers unloaded one of several machines full of the clothing of her shrieking progeny. Two dogs standing in the open doorway engaged in the wary sniffing that seems to be the canine equivalent of the human handshake.

The grocery store was shabby but respectable.

Custer's Last Stand, however, looked like nothing Aunt Charlotte had ever seen before or was ever likely to see again.

Its name was writ large in garish red letters of night-blooming neon on a sign above the door. The lower half of its plate-glass window was adorned with a plastic reproduction of green- and red-stained glass, above which only the heads and shoulders of customers on the tall bar stools showed like a line of busts chiseled by some mad sculptor.

In the front window hung a large, glittering square object which appeared to be made of ornately chased fool's gold. Set into its four sides were photographs of tavern scenes some twelve or fourteen inches high. The thing revolved slowly on its gilded chain so that each picture appeared in the window at about twenty-second intervals. Always amused by it before, Dinah saw it now as a representation of aggressive, almost exquisite bad taste.

Still viewing everything through Aunt Charlotte's eyes, as it were, she was acutely conscious of the dim, cavelike interior as she hurried through the door.

The bar was almost deserted at this early hour, yet its Gomorrhean atmosphere was ingrained. There were only five people inside Custer's Last Stand. John, the middle-aged black bartender, wore impeccable slacks, sport shirt, beret, and a look of amiable boredom.

A young man with long, wavy brown hair sat on a bar stool. Dressed in a tan fringed suede jacket, tan levis, and suede fringed boots, he looked not unlike General Custer himself. Beside him sat one of the neighborhood drunks, a short, slender youngish man with a look of stupefied intoxication. It was the way he always looked. Since he never spoke to anybody and nobody ever spoke to him, he had become a mystery figure, subject of speculation and rumor, the most bizarre of which was the claim by somebody or other that he worked in the news department of a TV station.

In a back booth sat an elderly man and woman gravely regarding a checkerboard on the red plastic table top between them. They were bespectacled and respectable, dressed conservatively in old but elegant clothes. Like their clothes, Amanda Prentiss and Ted Winthrop were well-preserved.

Amanda, in a Chanel-type suit, was slender and erect. She had vivid blue eyes and short hair, which looked somewhat like a white chrysanthemum. Ted was also white-haired, with the look of twinkly balminess of one of P. G. Wodehouse's elderly British peers.

"Good mornin', Miss Dinah. Hit sho is a pretty day, ain't it?" John was playing the role of old black Southern retainer, which usually evoked a spate of satirical banter with his more sophisticated customers.

Today, however, Dinah said absently, "Yes, a lovely day."

He walked to the far end of the bar, looking puzzled, as he watched her moving grimly toward the booth.

"Granny," gasped Dinah.

Amanda and Ted looked up at last from the checkerboard. Seeing her agitation, they began speaking at once. "My dear child," said Amanda. "What is it, Dinah?" Ted asked.

She slid into the seat beside her grandmother. "Telegram . . . Aunt Charlotte. Coming here today."

"You sound like a telegram yourself," said Ted. "Calm down and get your breath."

John lifted the hinged section at the end of the bar. Advancing on them at a dignified trot, he asked worriedly, "Is something the matter?"

"Something is," said Amanda. "What does this telegram say, Dinah?"

Dinah read her scribbled copy.

"Who is Charlotte?" asked John.

"A very good question," pronounced Amanda. "You might wonder why we are so disturbed at the prospect of a visit from this relative, or relative-in-law."

"Charlotte Prentiss is Amanda's sister-in-law," Ted told him. "Their late husbands were brothers."

"Oh, is that all?"

"With a sister-in-law like Charlotte, it is a great deal," snapped Amanda. "It's pretty involved and probably beyond the comprehension of a simple black man."

"Yes'm, but youall knows ah worries 'bout mah white folks," said John, reverting to his Southern darky role. "If youall can jes' splain it to me in words ah can understan'—"

Chapter Two

"My late husband, George Prentiss, invented a better bobbin in 1935," Amanda began. "He was no business man, though. His brother, Philip, who, within narrow limits, was pretty shrewd, took over the management of the bobbin. He did things like leasing it to textile mills all over the South instead of selling it outright, as George probably would have done."

She sighed and drank the last sip of sherry in her glass. "George trusted his brother. So in his will he left Philip in charge of the bobbin and everything else he had. While Philip was alive, he treated me fairly. His one weakness was that he trusted his wife, Charlotte, in the same naïve way that George had trusted him."

"Granny," Dinah broke in impatiently, "they're on the way. They could be arriving any minute now."

"In which case, time doesn't matter. There's nothing we can do."

"I don't like that attitude," Ted objected. "I like to think there's always something you can do."

"Me, too," said John. "But I still don't know why you're so upset."

Amanda stared into the empty glass as if it were a crystal ball. "Philip left everything to Charlotte, to dispense with as she saw fit. I was to get half the royalties from the bobbin. My heirs will continue to get it if I die before Charlotte. Tom Andrews, Charlotte's brother who was president of the Andrewsville bank, managed Philip's estate until he died a couple of years ago. Since then it's been managed by the bank, which is now run by Charlotte's three nephews, Tom Andrews' sons. The trick is that Charlotte can leave the bobbin to anybody she chooses. I imagine Philip thought that Tom Andrews would see that she did the right thing. But the estate is now being run by her nephews, whom I don't know very well."

"You should have contested that crazy will of your husband's," said John.

"Oh, I did. But in 1947 in South Carolina, women were considered incapable of handling money. Charlotte's men folks owned and operated the town and the bank, and the court decided she was more competent, or had access to competence. The judge actually referred to me as a 'lone widow woman' and Charlotte as a 'member of a family of financiers.'"

Dinah said angrily, "What he didn't know was that Charlotte's family is a matriarchy run by Charlotte."

"Now, my dear, we don't know that for a certainty," Ted protested. "Amanda just said she doesn't know the nephews very well."

"I think I begin to see your problem," said John, waving his arm in a gesture intended to encompass not only Custer's Last Stand but the entire neighborhood. "She won't be too impressed with the place where you live. But didn't you know she might come to see you sometime?"

"Charlotte," said Amanda, "decided about five years

ago that her arthritis was going to keep her at home for the rest of her life."

"Do you suppose she's found a new cure?" Ted speculated.

"I doubt it," said Amanda. "I think there's something she considers important enough to come here for."

"Is there any chance they haven't left yet?" asked Ted.

"I don't know," mused Amanda. "It's two hundred miles, and 'afternoon' covers a lot of hours."

"So if you can think of something to keep them from starting down here, you might call and head them off," John suggested.

"But what?" Amanda asked beseechingly. "It's too late to rent a house in the suburbs. But how about going to a motel because of a busted water heater flooding the house or a tree falling on it?"

"Or you could say one of you has something contagious," said John.

Amanda stood up. "That's a brilliant idea, John. Charlotte is not afraid of anything she can intimidate. Germs are among the few living creatures she fears and respects. You must be suitably rewarded, John," she announced grandly. "I shall do everything in my power to see that your race gets full equality."

John rolled his eyes and grinned. "Yes'm, Miss Amanda. We sho' does 'preciate dat. Yes'm, we does."

As the three of them rushed to the door, John called out, "Hey, what about your checker game?"

"Leave it," Amanda told him. "With luck, we'll be back in about thirty minutes. Without it, this saloon will be off limits to us for several days."

Pausing at the curb to look for oncoming traffic, she said, "Be thinking of diseases," and hurried across in front of a beer truck, leaving Ted and Dinah on the other side.

"How about pneumonia?" Ted shouted above the truck engine's roar as the driver parked in front of Custer's Last Stand.

"Too serious," she told him when he and Dinah reached the other side. "The patient would be in the hospital. We must have germs swarming around the house."

In the house, Amanda went to the phone, and Dinah followed Ted into the kitchen. "I can't bear to listen. I know they've left."

"Undoubtedly," he said calmly, holding the kettle under the hot-water faucet. "I think coffee will be needed, with perhaps a dollop of brandy."

Dinah left him puttering with instant coffee and a brandy bottle and went back in the hall as Amanda was hanging up the phone.

"They left an hour and a half ago," she said sadly.

Dinah patted her arm. "Come and sit down. Ted's bringing coffee with a dollop of brandy."

In the living room, Amanda sank down to the sofa.

"I think," said Dinah, "it's very likely she heard something about where you're living and decided to come down and see for herself."

Ted came in carrying a tray of coffee mugs. "Amanda, I don't like these big, ungainly mugs. What happened to your Worcester cups? I can't find them."

"Oh, for God's sake, Ted. You make me feel that story must be true about Nero's fiddling while Rome burned."

"They left an hour and a half ago," Dinah told him. "Which means we've had it."

"We have not, in your vulgar parlance, had it," Amanda declared pluckily. "We shall continue to think."

She picked up a mug of coffee. "Ted, did you put

brandy in here? And if so, how much? We've already had three glasses of sherry, and our cause will be even more hopeless if we're drunk when Charlotte gets here."

"Only a dollop," he assured her.

"What is a dollop, anyway? It sounds like one of those flexible words that can be all things to all people."

"Indeed," he said with a seraphic smile.

"Oh, stop it," said Dinah. "We don't have time for small talk."

"Why not?" asked Ted. "In a little while, they'll drive up here and see a neighborhood that could be an inspiring sight only to a sociologist studying urban problems. The anarchists, the winos, the Desperadoes, the Grass Menagerie, the Jesus Livers."

"Perhaps if she saw only a few of them at a time," Amanda ventured in a small, hopeless voice. "They don't all appear at once."

"Maybe it would be better if they did," said Dinah. "We could tell her it was a street festival—fertility rites or something."

They lapsed into silence at this appalling thought. Dinah had encountered the problem before with suburban friends seeing Midtown for the first time. Only about every third or fourth house had been remodeled or restored on Mimosa Way and surrounding streets, and the people living in the unrestored houses had a way of being dramatically conspicuous.

Next door on the north there was Ted's exquisitely restored house, considered to be one of the city's finest examples of Victoriana.

But next to him on the other side lived a little group of anarchists who had added nothing to the house except a black flag depending from a tall standard on the porch.

Along with the larger ideals of anarchy there seemed to be a scorn of such establishment practices as mowing yards and picking up beer cans and wine bottles. If this were the only house where inhabitants left yards in their natural state, they might be shrugged off as the neighborhood weirdos. But not in a neighborhood full of weirdos.

The winos worked in other people's yards but not their own. Five of them—three men and two women—lived in an old ruin of a Victorian house across and up the street in what was cynically called a furnished apartment by a landlord who lived in a neat suburb.

The front porch was also furnished, with a couple of broken-down sofas, bits and pieces of chairs, a broken television, and a stove and refrigerator that no longer worked. Arguments erupted frequently into fights, and from time to time more broken furniture appeared on the porch, giving the appearance to passers-by of a recent and sudden disaster—a fire or explosion, rather than gradual accretion.

Next door to the south of Amanda's house lived the Grass Menagerie, a rock-and-roll group numbering, most of the time, between fifteen and twenty, with children and husbands and wives, or mates, of the musicians.

Aunt Charlotte, Dinah reflected grimly, would take a particularly dim view of this bustling little commune, whose ideas of informal living were not at all the patio-and-grill concept of this term glorified in women's magazines.

But the Grass Menagerie were charming innocents compared to the occupants of two houses on Fern Terrace, a sadly misnamed street next to Mimosa Way.

They were the Desperadoes, a gang of bikers whose presence in the neighborhood united such widely divergent groups as anarchists and architects in a common cause. The Desperadoes must go—to jail, to California, to another neighborhood—along with the owners of the two houses, who lived, of course, in the suburbs.

"I have a vague idea," said Ted.

"Vagueness is no detriment right now," said Amanda. "We have a little time to shape it up and bring it into focus. Speak."

"Well, I've been thinking that the one thing Charlotte loves and respects above all else is money. We know this property is a damned good investment, although it's hard for outsiders to see it now."

Amanda favored him with a benign smile. "Of course. How clever of you, Ted. And yours is an authoritative voice on real estate."

Ted was retired from the Winthrop Realty Company. Amanda had worked for him as an agent for twelve years and retired when Ted's nephew, David, had taken over the business.

Ted, thought Dinah, was looking almost insufferably pleased with himself as he said, "Show her that book and the newspaper articles about the trend to move to old downtown neighborhoods and fix up old houses. Tell her about the Midtown Neighborhood Association. I'll chime in and say I saw it coming and bought the house next door six years ago."

"That will help, all right," said Dinah. "But Aunt Charlotte is one of those people who will see only what's here now. I've got several friends like that, and so have you. The sight of this place really freaks them out."

Amanda said, "Dinah, as a writer and editorial assistant of a small but dignified magazine, you shock me when you sully your speech with such slang."

"Sorry, Granny. I'll try to remember to unsully my speech around you."

"And Charlotte." Amanda pressed a hand to her brow. "Dear God, how quickly we can become obsessed with Charlotte again. It seems much more outrageous after five years of rest from her."

She sat up and took a sip of coffee. "I don't know how much brandy you put in here, but I'm beginning to feel a lot more sanguine about the whole thing."

Dinah said, "The border line between sanguine and drunk has never been determined, but I understand that experiments are being made with volunteers found in bars after midnight. So," she said, getting to her feet, "I'm going to pour this out and drink some straight coffee. Someone must be sober when they get here."

"What a prig you've made of this girl," Ted complained. "Of course you can't pour out good brandy. Leave it here and your grandmother and I will divide it."

"While you strategists are planning the big campaign, someone must attend to K.P. I've got to run to the grocery store and buy twice as much food for the weekend. You can make the beds and get rooms ready for them, Granny."

"Oh, no," said Amanda. "We're not going to be left here alone to greet Charlotte. Ted and I will go to the grocery store while you stay here and make beds."

Dinah said crossly, "Oh, all right. We don't have time to argue. I'll stay, but if you're going, go now."

Ted rose to his feet somewhat unsteadily and said in a declamatory voice, "Or, as someone else put it even more aptly, 'If it were done when 'tis done, then 'twere well it were done quickly.'"

Chapter Three

Dinah came back from the kitchen to see Amanda and Ted walking out the front door, giggling and whispering, and remembered, with fresh dismay, that Saturday was their drinking afternoon, spent usually in Custer's Last Stand where the two old dears would get what they quaintly called "tipsy." About seven, they would leave to have dinner at Amanda's or Ted's, or if they weren't too tipsy, a restaurant.

After they had retired from the real estate business, they had opened an antique and junk shop in a derelict old house of Ted's on Monroe Drive, four blocks away. Dinah considered the shop a Godsend; it kept them happily occupied and out of mischief all week. The shop was closed on Tuesdays so they could replenish the stock with trips to auctions, junk shops, and wrecking companies' junkyards, accompanied by one or two winos to load heavy things into Ted's station wagon.

The surprising thing about the shop was that they were making money out of it. Or not so surprising, actually, when you remembered that beneath their flighty eccentricities were a couple of pretty shrewd brains.

Dinah had argued many times that it wouldn't be financial catastrophe if Charlotte left the bobbin rights to her relatives. But the ancient injustice had never ceased to rankle. Amanda maintained it was not only the principal, but also the interest.

About half the things in the house had been found in junk forays. Looking around at some of it as she picked up the tray, Dinah reflected that it made an interesting but somewhat unco-ordinated decor; an unintentional achievement of the new "undecorated look."

There were the Chinese Chippendale sofa and coffee table bought at an estate sale, an assortment of Empire, Victorian, Queen Anne, and 1920 French chairs and tables, and an impressive collection of Satsuma, Imari, and rose medallion vases, lamps, bowls, and teapots—less impressive on close examination because of cracks and chips, euphemistically called "age lines" in auction lists. Chinese and persian rugs, fine but worn, covered portions of the heart-pine floors in the living room, dining room, and long central hall.

The house had been an Edwardian ruin when they bought it two years ago after Amanda's house in Morningside had been condemned because it was in the path of a proposed expressway.

Ted had told her about the vacant house next door to him, for sale cheap but in such deplorable condition that restoration would double the price. The elderly former owner had turned the back bedroom and back hallway into a tiny efficiency apartment. Amanda had called it "a place we can rent out if we fall on evil times." But until evil times arrived it was occupied by Dinah, providing separate living quarters combined with the togetherness of living in the same house.

The front bedroom was Amanda's and the middle one a

guest room. But one guest room is not enough for guests of different sexes requiring separate rooms. So she'd have to give up her snuggery and move to a day bed on the back porch.

The enclosed porch was separated from the kitchen by an old-fashioned door with plate-glass inset in the upper half, through which the occupant of the day bed was exposed to the view and conversational gambits of people in the kitchen. She bleakly decided to hang a curtain on the door before she went to bed.

Aunt Charlotte would have the middle room next to Amanda's, and Clifford could stay in her little apartment. Reluctantly, she took a stack of linens to get her living quarters ready for what she could only think of as an interloper.

She had seen Clifford three or four times, the last when she was eleven and he was thirteen, an indeterminate age when personality, character, and appearance are almost embryonic. She remembered that he had been tall for his age and going through a phase of intense shyness, as she had been. Aunt Charlotte had brought Clifford down for a week during the summer.

Amanda's attempts to coerce Dinah into being a good hostess were sad failures. Dinah and Clifford would leave the house together to go to a movie, or a neighbor's picnic or swimming pool party, walk silently along together until they arrived, and then separate to join clusters of their own sex.

All she really knew about him was that he was the youngest of the triumvirate of Charlotte's nephews who ran the Andrewsville bank. Dinah had never known any bankers and never wanted to know any. Bankers were about as far removed from her little circle as Hottentots.

Her bed-sitting room seemed already to have lost its inviolacy as she made up one of her window-seat beds with clean sheets, leaving the other bare beneath its turquoise spread.

Glancing around for things that should be removed for an alien presence, she picked up a letter from a boy friend in New Orleans and plucked from the bookcase a paperback copy of *The Joy of Sex*.

The room began to take on the remoteness of possessions about to be wrested from us. She looked at it through a sort of double vision, her own heightened awareness of familiar objects mingled with the projected impression it might make on a stuffy young banker. Handicapped, however, by total ignorance of young bankers, she left off speculating and hurried through her chores.

Ted and Amanda came back while she was making up the Victorian guest-room bed for Aunt Charlotte.

She found them bustling around the kitchen, so cheerfully and playfully she wondered if they'd stopped somewhere for a drink. Ted was beside the table, rummaging in sacks and throwing plastic-wrapped meats and vegetables to Amanda, standing beside the open refrigerator. Some she caught and some fell to the floor.

"It's three-thirty," Dinah announced.

"We'll just have time for a glass of sherry, Ted," said Amanda.

"Before what?"

"Why, before they get here, of course," chirped Amanda. "We bought a nice big pot roast you can just pop into the oven while we pop into the living room and sit down and catch our breath."

"Aunt Charlotte is the one who's going to catch your

breath," Dinah said sourly. "She'll be knocked out by the fumes."

Her plea was hopeless. Ted was already fussing with wine glasses and sherry bottle while Dinah looked on with tight-lipped censure.

"Talk about the generation gap," he said chattily. "I think the Puritan work ethic is making a distressingly strong comeback among the young. They don't know how to relax and have fun."

"Nobody can have fun with Aunt Charlotte around," Dinah pointed out. "It's a matter of degree of unpleasantness."

Ted handed Amanda a wine glass and picked up his own. "Then we shall have as much fun as we can before she gets here."

Dinah sighed and bent down to pick up the roast, one of the packages Amanda had failed to catch when Ted threw it across the room.

As she was closing the oven door on the roast and assorted vegetables, Amanda called, "They're here."

Dinah hurried through the hall to stand with Amanda and Ted, looking out the front door.

A powder-blue Cadillac had drawn up in front of the house. Parked between Dinah's 1955 Ford and the tie-dyed blue van streaked with gray which transported the Grass Menagerie around the country, it looked, she thought, like the King's chariot on its rounds among the peasantry.

Aunt Charlotte and Clifford stood beside it on the grass verge between street and sidewalk, staring apprehensively up at the house as if they were thinking they were at the wrong address.

"Charlotte is a formidable figure of a woman," whispered Ted.

"A dreadnaught," said Amanda. "Or juggernaut."

Aunt Charlotte, in a gray suit and shirt-style blouse, was tall and big-boned, her large nose and square jaw, if not handsome, at least rather imposing. In a charcoal suit, Clifford was tall, dark, handsome, and bankerish.

While they stood hesitantly—indeed fearfully—looking around, Mimosa Way was outdoing itself in an extravaganza of seamy eccentricity.

Two of the worst looking of the neighborhood winos were making their inebriated way down the sidewalk within a couple of feet of Charlotte and Clifford.

To Dinah, Mrs. Prather had always looked more fey than drunk, with a vague, beatific smile, long, flowing red hair, and a layered look of clothing—butcher apron over blue jeans, gray short-sleeved blouse over purple long-sleeved blouse. Her companion was Tim Dobson, who affected white overalls which must have been left over from some former employment as a painter or carpenter.

Aunt Charlotte's astonished gaze did not linger on them; it shifted to a wispy youth with the long hair and yellow velvet robe of the Jesus Lives Sect.

He appeared to be floating rather than walking, following closely on the heels of the derelicts, the three of them looking like allegorical figures in a Victorian painting representing contrasting conditions of the human soul—like Degradation and Redemption.

As Charlotte and Clifford watched the little procession in awe probably tinged with horror, a couple of bearded college students in a seedy duplex across the street decided to relax with their childlike hobby of throwing lighted firecrackers into the yard.

When the first fusillade went off, Clifford grabbed Aunt Charlotte's shoulders and pulled her down against the car door in the mistaken—but understandable—impression that someone was shooting at them.

After the explosions continued for half a minute with no apparent injuries to cars or people, Clifford raised his head to peer through the car windows at the students.

He said something to Aunt Charlotte and they scrambled to their feet, once more turning to look up at the house. Aunt Charlotte saw them in the doorway.

"Here we are, Charlotte," Amanda called gaily.

Chapter Four

Aunt Charlotte and Amanda greeted each other with the classic sister-in-law embrace, placing their hands on each other's shoulders, gingerly touching cheeks, and quickly backing off.

"My dear, you're looking well," Aunt Charlotte observed in her booming contralto.

"And so are you. You appear to be in very good health. How is your arthritis?"

"Much better. I have a new doctor."

They moved into the house, which Aunt Charlotte declared to be, "So charming and quaint, my dear."

"Thank you. You'll want to go to your rooms first, I know. Dinah will show you while Ted and I make coffee. Or would you rather have tea or Coke, Charlotte?"

"Coffee would be lovely," declared Aunt Charlotte.

Walking ahead of them down the long hall, Dinah was puzzled and uneasy about Aunt Charlotte's failure to comment on the neighborhood, an omission somewhat like ignoring a South American street riot, and which showed, Dinah was sure, that she had already heard about it.

Clifford left Aunt Charlotte and her suitcase in the middle bedroom, and Dinah took him across the hall to her apartment.

He set down his suitcase and looked around. "This is yours, isn't it, Dinah?"

"Yes, but I have a comfortable place to sleep."

"Where?" he was regarding her with dark eyes which would have aroused a certain amount of interest if they had belonged to anybody else.

"A day bed on the back porch."

"I'll sleep on the day bed."

Dinah smiled. "You don't want to make me feel inhospitable?"

"Certainly not. Last thing in the world I'd want to do."

She noticed his mouth quirking and looked at him with quickened interest. This was not the Clifford she remembered.

"You've grown a lot since I last saw you," she said.

"And so have you." His glance moved from her face downward. "Just enough in just the right places."

"Thank you, sir. I'd better go help Ted and Amanda. You'd like a drink?"

"I would indeed, as soon as I get out of my banker's clothes and into something comfortable."

In the kitchen, Amanda was saying, "What a splendid idea. A pitcher of martinis sounds very nice for this time of day, Ted."

"Aunt Charlotte doesn't drink martinis," Dinah said repressively. "As I recall, she asked for coffee."

She lowered her voice, "Listen, Granny, Aunt Charlotte is up to something. Did you think it a little strange she didn't say anything about this neighborhood, about the parade of residents, and those firecrackers which they obviously thought were gunshots fired by bearded revolutionaries? Does that suggest to you that she already knew about the neighborhood and was startled only by the actual sight of it coming on so strong?"

"So?" Amanda challenged, with the insouciance built on a solid base of alcoholic fortification. "We had figured it was probably something like that."

"And way back then, about one o'clock, we also figured we'd better watch our step and find out why she came down here so suddenly. So, I say you'd better stick with sherry or switch to coffee."

She looked up to see Clifford standing in the doorway, dressed in gray slacks and a navy knit sport shirt which looked pretty sensational with his dark hair and eyes. Wondering how long he'd been standing there, she reminded herself sternly that he was the enemy, and she had a sneaking idea she'd have to keep reminding herself.

He came into the room. "May I help?"

"Oh, yes," Amanda told him, "if you know how to make martinis."

"Bankers know how to make good martinis."

He was looking at Dinah, mocking her snobbery, knowing instinctively exactly what she thought of bankers.

"We're a dull, cloddish lot," he went on. "Junior Chamber of Commerce and right-wing Republican rallies. But we do know how to make martinis."

"Then you shall do it, my boy," said Ted, adding virtuously, "I'm mostly a sherry drinker, myself."

Dinah made instant coffee for Aunt Charlotte, and found her in the living room, examining the mark on an old Crown Derby plate.

"Oh, the coffee smells good. And you look very good, my dear. You've grown into quite an attractive young lady."

Something about her tone suggested surprise at this development, yet her attitude and everything she'd said sounded as if she were enrolled in a charm school and had got maybe halfway through the course.

Portentous, thought Dinah as she thanked her.

"I suppose most of these lovely things came from Amanda's shop. I'd like to go there and look around."

"I know she'd love to take you over there."

The combination of Amanda and Ted and a pitcher of martinis sent her scurrying back to the kitchen with the respectable excuse of looking at the roast.

Amanda and Ted and Clifford were gathered around the martini pitcher, sampling and pronouncing it good—very good indeed.

Clifford poured one for her and she took a couple of quick gulps, on the theory that whatever was going to happen would be far less jarring to a fuzzy brain than a clear one. Two more swallows and she began to wonder if she might be able to get some information out of Clifford when she found a chance to be alone with him. And in a burst of honesty added, "Who do you think you're kidding? You want to be alone with him solely for the purpose of being alone with him."

The martinis the others took to the living room were refills, so she poured another for herself and followed them.

Knowing Aunt Charlotte's views about any sort of alcohol taken internally, Dinah was even more apprehensive when she ignored the martinis and told Amanda and Ted she wanted to see their shop.

Amanda was at the stage of intoxication marked by exaggerated dignity and graciousness. "We'd love to take you there tomorrow." She took a ladylike sip of her martini. "It's sort of chaotic right now. Several shipments we haven't had time to go through yet."

Shipments, thought Dinah, was an inaccurate choice of words for the towering piles of junk in the derelict old house. But Aunt Charlotte's curious new tact would probably extend to this eyesore, too.

Conversation languished and died. It occurred to Dinah later that nature really does abhor a vacuum, for into the silence new sounds erupted from next door—a tuning up of musical instruments on the front porch. The Grass Menagerie.

At first the noise was subdued, a desultory twanging of electric guitars. Then the volume increased to a pulsating clamor. A young man's voice bawled into the afternoon stillness. "I'm gonna get me a new baby, I'm gonna get me a new baby—"

Dinah had heard it before and paid little attention. Repetition had robbed the words of meaning. Thus she was as surprised as anybody when after about the fifth "Gonna get me a new baby" the singer ended with "Cause my old one's got the—" and here, musicians and singers joined in a clapping of hands.

She looked around. Clifford had caught it all right. Amanda and Ted sat perfectly still, staring straight ahead. Aunt Charlotte looked puzzled.

There was no hope that it wouldn't be repeated. This time the voice was louder and more agitated. "Yes, gonna get me a new baby, cause my old one's got the—" clap, clap, clap.

She saw comprehension dawning on Aunt Charlotte's face. Aunt Charlotte had worked for several years with what she called "wayward girls" and taught a Sunday school class of boys in a mill workers' neighborhood. In

Aunt Charlotte's class and generation, it was obligatory for ladies to devote a certain amount of time to good works.

Why didn't somebody say something? She racked her brain, but chit-chat was simply too feeble to be pitted against such overwhelming competition.

Clifford got up, walked into the dining room and turned on the window air conditioner. "Seems warm in here. Maybe it's the martinis."

It broke the spell. Everybody started talking at once about different things. Ted about the unseasonable warmth, Amanda about the treasures in their shop. Aunt Charlotte began a discourse on day lilies, which had the facile glibness of an oft-repeated garden club speech.

The air conditioner's busy thrum didn't drown out the music, only the words, repeating the medically sound but conversationally unfortunate reason for getting a new baby.

Then a new sound was added—one which blended so fittingly with the wailing next door that at first Dinah thought it was part of the music. It drew closer and became separate and distinct—the shriek of a police siren.

It seemed to be a couple of blocks away, but the chances of a random police car turning into Mimosa Way were always quite good. And so it did this time, the siren diminishing to a throaty growl out front.

"Police!" bleated Aunt Charlotte, forgetting her policy of ignoring the neighborhood activities.

"Just someone complaining about the noise next door," Amanda said with a gay little laugh. "A musical group, and quite successful, I understand. A couple of their records have become best sellers with the young people."

The wailing and strumming stopped. A man's voice said,

"You kids know better than to practice out here. We get a couple of calls on it every time."

"But it's hot inside, officer." This was a fluting female voice Dinah recognized as that of Jane Walker, owner of the house and leader of the rock group.

"Get an air conditioner," the policeman told her. "We got too much to do around here to be wasting time on this kind of complaint."

Aunt Charlotte, looking alarmed, put down her cup and leaned forward. "What does he mean 'too much to do around here'?"

Amanda looked her in the eye and said, "I really don't know. Would anyone like a drink?"

"Not right now, thank you," said Clifford. "Dinah, do you need help in the kitchen?"

"Yes, indeed," she assured him, reflecting that he was also contriving to be alone with her, but for a different reason. She wanted to work the conversation around to Aunt Charlotte's purpose in coming here. At least, she amended, that was her primary reason for wanting to be alone with him. If there were secondary ones, she preferred not to go into them just yet.

Aunt Charlotte asked if there was time for her to take a bath and a short nap before dinner. Amanda said, a shade too hastily, that there was plenty of time.

"Let's go back to the first question," said Ted. "The one about would anybody like a drink."

Chapter Five

Dinah couldn't remember ever sitting through a more uncomfortable meal. In trying to act sober, Amanda and Ted were pompous and formal.

Aunt Charlotte, who usually behaved like the Red Queen, was still exuding the strange charm which made Dinah so uneasy. Since she still hadn't mentioned the neighborhood, there had been no chance for the real estate speech Ted and Amanda had planned so carefully.

Before dinner, Dinah and Clifford had sat at the kitchen table, chopping and peeling ingredients for a tossed salad and drinking a martini. She was forced to admit to herself that Clifford was not stuffy and dull. On the contrary, he was witty and urbane, expert at the sort of nonsensical banter that was also a specialty of Dinah and her friends. Despite the instant camaraderie, she hadn't got up the nerve to ask him the reason for Aunt Charlotte's visit.

Now she was concentrating on getting away from all of them and over to the meeting across the street.

Finally, over coffee, an uncompanionable clinking of spoons and clicking of cups, she said with elaborate casualness, "I'm afraid I'll have to leave the dishes for you, Amanda, or I'll be late to the meeting."

"Girls are so busy with community affairs these days," Aunt Charlotte pried adroitly.

When no one responded, she tried again, "Or is it a social club?"

"More like that," Dinah said vaguely.

"It's the Intellectual Society of the South," Amanda announced grandly and somewhat bibulously.

"Oh, how interesting. I don't believe I've ever heard of it, though."

Amanda said, "It's a local organization of writers and editors."

It seemed a perfect example to Dinah of how it is possible to tell the truth and yet create an entirely false impression.

Emboldened by gin and her own duplicity, Amanda said, "Possibly Clifford would like to go, dear."

Dinah took a sip of coffee and avoided looking at Clifford across the table.

"I'm sure he would," trilled Aunt Charlotte. "Clifford loves to read. He reads all sorts of books."

"All sorts," echoed Clifford.

Dinah smiled at him. "We'd like very much to have you."

"I'd like very much to go if visitors are welcome."

"Oh, yes, it's actually very informal. A lot of the members bring visitors."

"Where is this meeting?" asked Aunt Charlotte.

"At a sort of community center near here," said Dinah.

Clifford asked the question again a few minutes later on the front porch.

"Well, as a matter of fact, it's across the street."

"The grocery store and launderette seem to be closed, so I gather it's the bar."

"Custer's Last Stand is a sort of community center," she said defensively.

Clifford laughed and took her hand. "I don't doubt it. And I'm immensely relieved. I was looking forward to an evening of Socratic discussion or poetry reading. Tell me about your intellectual society."

"Pseudo-Intellectual," Dinah told him as they walked down the steps. "It's what you might call a loosely knit organization. I wasn't kidding when I said it was informal."

On the other side of the street, the Saturday night sounds of Custer's Last Stand assaulted the serenity of the moonlit night—a babble of voices, a juke box blaring out some still unidentifiable tune.

Outside the door, Clifford stared at the revolving gilded thing in the window and the heads showing above the plastic stained glass. He opened the door, releasing the full volume of bedlam with musical accompaniment and the universal barroom essence of alcohol, cigarette smoke, and numerous colognes, perfumes, and after-shave lotions borne on a blast of cold air.

The place was crowded with what must have been a bewildering assortment to Clifford—a sprinkling of well-dressed people among the tattered winos, over-alled ancients, and blue-jeaned, unisex young.

"Are all these people members of the Intellectual Society?" Clifford shouted in her ear.

"No, they'll be in the back. Keep going. Don't slow down or we might be trampled."

She dodged and pushed her way through clots of people to a gathering of a dozen or so seated around a long table pushed against a banquette.

A bearded man in sport shirt and levis saw them and beckoned.

"Clifford," said Dinah, "this is my boss, Miles Dennis, editor of *The Southern Conservationist*. My cousin, Clifford Andrews."

Dinah put her arm around the shoulder of a fragile-looking little old lady. She was Gillian Jones, a sociologist who wrote enormously popular books on mores and morals with case histories that sounded like alternating excerpts from Krafft-Ebing, and *True Confessions*.

She introduced Gilly to Clifford and looked up to see David Winthrop approaching. David's clothes were casual but not sloppy; his blond hair was cut in a modish Dutch boy length acceptable in downtown office and Midtown bar.

Introducing them, Dinah wondered bleakly how two men can instantly identify each other as rivals for the same girl.

"How do you do," said David stiffly. "I'll get some chairs."

Dinah remembered now that when they had arranged to sit together at the meeting David had said, "And we can go some place else afterward."

She waved at the people in the banquette and introduced Clifford to a couple of people sitting near them; Tom Cauldon of *Newsweek* and Betty Hines, a stunning blonde who had her own TV talk show.

David came back with a chair for Clifford. He set it down next to Betty Hines, gave Dinah a triumphant smirk, and left again. Clifford sat down next to Betty Hines; Dinah sat between Clifford and Gillian.

Gillian said in a low voice, "Looks like you got your dates mixed up and are about to lose both of them. But only temporarily, my dear. Men like to think they've beat out a lot of competition by the time they finally get you in bed."

"Can't you ever think of anything but sex, Gilly?" Dinah said irritably.

"Actually I'm a sweet little old lady who should be at home tatting antimacassars and growing African violets. I've been forced into the role of a senile Scheherazade in order to sell books. Sex goes over big with the women's clubs."

"You're not talking to a woman's club now," said Dinah. "You're talking to me."

"I was trying out that bit about the antimacassars and African violets on you. Do you think they'd like it?"

Dinah considered. "Maybe if they knew absolutely nothing about you except that stuff on the jacket blurbs. Why don't you try it in some place far off like Butte, Montana, where they'll be putting you on a plane right after the lecture."

"African violets may be a little out of character," Gilly admitted. "The only house plant I've ever had any luck with was that Dieffenbachia that grew up to the ceiling."

"There you are, then. You'd be the first to say, 'Never pretend to be something you're not.'"

"The first to say it and the last to do it," said Gillian. "You need a drink."

"Waiter," Gilly yelled at a long-haired boy distinguishable from the other long-haired boys by a butcher's apron. He drifted over.

"I'll have the same; Jack Daniel and water."

Dinah said she'd have Bourbon and water and got Clifford's attention by digging her elbow viciously into his ribs. He turned away from the beautiful Betty and looked at her as if she were someone he'd met at a large party and couldn't quite place.

"Your order," she said frostily. "What do you want to drink?"

"Oh. Scotch and soda. And what," he said with simpering solicitude, "would you like, Betty?"

"I hope she doesn't tell him," Gillian said in a harsh whisper. "He looks too square a young man to hear obscenities from the lips of young ladies. What does he do?"

"He's a banker."

"Good God, you shouldn't have brought him to a place like this."

"He seems to be having a good time," Dinah remarked acidly.

She looked up to see David approaching with a drink and folding chair.

"No room, no room," cried Gilly.

Dinah smiled at him. "'There's plenty of room,' said Alice. Sit here between me and the Mad Tatter."

Gilly gave a raucous laugh and slapped the palm of her hand on the table.

Tom Cauldon, on the other side of Gilly, patted her shoulder. "Gilly, love, you've accidently called the meeting to order. What a shame. We'll be forced to bring up business, and a damned serious business it is, too."

He stood up. "Ladies and gentlemen, in the absence of your president, I am your permanent temporary chairman.

"I'm sure most of you have either forgotten or were not informed of the purpose of our meeting tonight. The last quarter of the year is upon us, and in the absence of the revolving committee, we must call on the members to vote on the recipient of our Able and Noble Teacher Award.

"I shall explain briefly for those who have missed the

last ten meetings and others who weren't paying attention.

"In the last year or so, with a couple of months off for good behavior, P.I.S.S. has given an Able and Noble Teacher Award—P.I.S.S.A.N.T.—to the person, or personage, who during that quarter has made what we consider to be the most profound or worthwhile public statement."

He paused to take a sip of his drink. "Are there any nominations?"

Gilly stood up. "Just a second, Gilly. I haven't recognized you yet."

Miles Dennis said, "I move we adjourn until the chairman is sober enough to recognize members."

Tom ignored him. "The chair recognizes Gillian Jones, author of *Sublimation and Sanctimony* and other salacious works."

Gilly said, "Thank you, Mr. Chairman, if indeed you are our chairman, I wish to nominate Dr. Marjorie Bead, the noted anthropologist, for a statement which appeared in her column in the October issue of *Ladies Home Guide*.

She fished around in a capacious black handbag and pulled out a page torn from a magazine.

"Dr. Bead says here: 'In our society, most women seem to be content with the housewife role. Although this is not true in other cultures I have studied, they are uncivilized people who have no refrigerators or wall-to-wall carpet to keep clean or car pools to school and Cub Scout meetings. The fact remains that someone must do these things, and the role of housewife has a long tradition behind it in our culture.'

"I scarcely need to point out to you that Dr. Bead herself has never been a housewife, although she was married for a good many years, and would be highly insulted if somebody told her to quit fooling around with this anthropology stuff and get on home where she's supposed to be and start baking some cakes."

The women cheered and the men booed.

"Thank you, Gilly," said Tom. "Anyone else?"

A slender, bearded young man stood up. Tom said, "The chair recognizes Leonard Pool, reporter and feature writer on the *Atlanta Journal*."

"I would like to nominate the Reverend Willie Cracker, the famous evangelist, for a statement in his syndicated column last Friday.

"The Reverend Cracker writes, 'It is a foolish mistake to say that our President is any more crooked or sneaky than any other politician. Every politician—indeed our entire society—is crooked and sneaky, and it is time for this nation to return to God.'"

Clifford whispered, "What am I offered not to tell Aunt Charlotte about P.I.S.S.?"

"You are offered nothing. I will not submit to blackmail."

"I meant no harm. I was only going to ask you to go on a picnic tomorrow."

"In that case, I accept."

He started talking to Betty again, and Dinah figured it was time she did some fence mending with David, who was now sulking silently beside her.

She decided to be forthright. "Where did you have in mind going after the meeting?" she said in what she hoped was a seductive whisper.

"No place in particular—I thought we might just drive around. But what about your large cousin?"

"He doesn't have to go everywhere with me. He came

down with Aunt Charlotte. An unexpected visit. We didn't know about it till today."

All he said was "Oh, I see." But he relaxed and smiled at her, making her feel somewhat deceitful because she had neglected to tell him that Clifford wasn't really kin to her.

Tom Cauldon was banging his glass on the table. "One motion at a time, please. You, Mr. Everhart, are a visitor, not a member, and you cannot second motions—or motion seconds, in the case of a duel."

Dinah punched Clifford in the ribs, which wasn't too polite but seemed the only way to get his attention away from his conversation with Betty.

Ted and Amanda stood in the doorway looking around.

"What have they done with Aunt Charlotte?" Clifford asked in a low voice.

Dinah stood up. "I'll find out." To David she said, "Back in a minute," which later proved to be a monumental misstatement. David stood up, too. "I'll escort you to the bar. I've got to go out and get my checkbook out of the glove compartment so I can pay the help here."

Amanda and Ted were sitting on bar stools when Dinah reached their side. Amanda was saying, "What was that nice new drink you were telling me about, Ted?"

In the tone of a stern parent speaking to a wayward child, Dinah said, "What have you done with Aunt Charlotte?"

Amanda jumped and turned to face her. "Please don't sneak up on me and make silly accusations like that. We haven't done anything with Charlotte. She took herself off to bed."

"Did she know you were coming over here?"

"Of course not. We didn't mention it till after she went to her room."

"You must stop harassing your grandmother while she's having a short respite from Charlotte," Ted reprimanded. "Is Clifford enjoying your meeting?"

Dinah considered. "Certain aspects of it, yes, but I don't think he's ever been to a meeting like it before."

Her glance wandered to the door, which was opening to reveal two people on the threshold.

One was a man about twenty-five to thirty, with a leonine head, long, tawny hair, and drooping mustache. He was dressed all in black—black levis, black boots, black T-shirt, and fringed black jacket.

The effect on the merrymakers was somewhat like that of the Red Death on the revelers at the masked ball. People stopped talking and looked. The atmosphere quivered with wariness.

Beside him was Aunt Charlotte. Dinah's first thought—that they had simply arrived at the door at the same time—was obviously wrong. Aunt Charlotte was talking to him. He answered her in a low voice, appearing polite and respectful.

"The leader of the Desperadoes," said Dinah in a faint whisper.

Ted said, "My God!"

Chapter Six

Charlotte said something else to the black-clad biker and he gave her a tentative little smile, oddly deferential.

The three at the bar had been stunned into speechlessness, watching Charlotte looking around, spying them, speaking again to the Desperado, and striding away from him toward the bar.

She spoke in the resonant contralto of Charlotte, the juggernaut, all traces of her new charm obliterated. "Amanda, there is a frightful disturbance going on next door to your house. Several fights or one large fight, I can't determine which."

"Charlotte," bleated Amanda in a small voice, "do you know that—ah—person you were talking to?"

"Artie? Of course I know him. He used to be in my Sunday school class. I was puzzled to see him in that odd-looking get-up and said so. I couldn't get much sense out of him about it—claimed it's the uniform of some sort of club he belongs to."

Her glance swept the room. "This is the most disreputable place I have ever seen, Amanda. I'm surprised to see you not only frequenting such a place yourself but allowing your granddaughter in here."

Her sharp-eyed gaze came to rest on Dinah. "Is your meeting over? Where is Clifford?"

"Clifford is . . ." Dinah began weakly, and looked up to see him pushing his way toward them.

"Aunt Charlotte," he said in a tone which indicated that he had decided to take the offensive, "what on earth are you doing here?"

"I might well ask you the same question, young man. You and Dinah left the house to go to a meeting of something called the Intellectual Society of the South at a community center."

"So we did, and this is it," Clifford said, grinning. "The society is meeting right back there—at that table pulled up to the booth—voting on an important matter."

"Clifford, you have deceived me, and not for the first time," she pronounced with biblical wrath. "Now you are adding mockery to deception."

"No, I'm not putting you on," he said mildly. "This is a sort of community center, as Dinah said."

"God help the community that uses this sinkhole of depravity as a gathering place."

"Spoken like an authentic saloon-wrecker," Clifford remarked approvingly. "Carrie Nation herself couldn't have put it better."

She glared at him. "Clifford, you've been drinking."

"So I have. I'd venture to say that everyone in here has been drinking. And if I may interrupt your temperance lecture, what in God's name were you doing with that biker?"

"Biker? That explains his strange costume, then, if he belongs to a group of bicycle enthusiasts. But he said he was—" she broke off.

Amanda made a strangled noise in her throat. Ted gave a short, barking laugh. Dinah and Clifford giggled.

Amanda changed the subject, or rather shifted it to another facet of the neighborhood activities. "Charlotte dropped over to tell us that there's a disturbance going on at the Grass Menagerie's house," she said in the chatty tones of someone reporting a social event. "Did you call the police, Charlotte?"

"I did not. It's your house and your duty to call the police."

Once again, the distant keening of police sirens increased in volume as they drew nearer.

"Someone seems to have beat you to it," Clifford remarked. "You'd better let me take you home, Aunt Charlotte. Would you like to go, Dinah? We can come back when things quiet down over there."

Charlotte went with them docilely and without protest, motioning good-by to Artie with that imperious wave halfway between greeting and benediction which royalty affects in public appearances. Probably, Clifford said later, because she was tired and sleepy, and most of the fight had gone out of her.

The fight, however, had not gone out of others in the neighborhood. They had picked an unfortunate moment to emerge from the bar.

The fight was spilling over into the street. One of the antagonists, in purple pants and checkered poncho, was teetering on the opposite curb, almost falling over backward into the street. He was shouting, "Come and get me, m—f—" and other crudities which Dinah and Clifford, on either side of Aunt Charlotte, tried to drown out by yelling reassurances into both of her ears about the playful nature of the fight—assertions belied by the melee on the front porch.

Several people appeared to be grappling in hand-to-hand combat while others preferred the less-intimate warfare of hurled missiles—beer cans, wine bottles, and chairs. Girls were screaming and men were bellowing, and added to the frightful din were the approaching sirens. Two police cars turned into Mimosa Way at the top of the hill in the next block, sped down the hill, and stopped at the house next door.

Aunt Charlotte, reaching the safety zone of Amanda's front steps, decided to stay and watch until the last of the Menagerie was shoved into the back of a paddy wagon, which had arrived as reinforcement a couple of minutes after the police cars.

As the last of the police vehicles departed into the night, Clifford sighed gustily in a silence which still seemed to be reverberating. "Ah, what a peaceful, almost pastoral scene. Look at the full moon shining through the leaves of yonder oak tree."

"Clifford, the more I see of you, the more convinced I am that you are drunk," declared Aunt Charlotte. "I shall be forced to speak to your older brother about your conduct."

"And he will say, 'Am I my brother's keeper?' And the answer is 'Certainly not.' He has quite enough responsibility running the bank and the Rotary Club and assorted charities."

"Hummph," said Aunt Charlotte, giving up.

She yawned ostentatiously. "Well, I'm going to bed. I'm not accustomed to such goings-on."

"I should hope not," said Clifford piously.

Dinah let Aunt Charlotte in with her key. Clifford took her hand and led her over to the swing.

"I don't want to seem critical of your neighborhood, Dinah, but that biker Aunt Charlotte was hob-nobbing with . . ."

"Used to be in her Sunday school class," she reminded him.

"Not one of her spectacular successes in Christian Living. But the thing is that she's too naïve to be allowed to roam loose around here. You see, she is accustomed to regarding thugs as social problems. And with the arrogance of the small-town big shot, she thinks no one would have the effrontery to do her bodily harm."

Dinah said, "He seems to be intimidated by her, though."

"Everyone is," said Clifford glumly.

During this exchange, his arm had gone around her shoulder, casually. And casualness, thought Dinah with inebriated detachment, was not the best approach. She wondered how he was going to make the conversational leap from Aunt Charlotte to passion.

There was a long silence. The swing creaked. Muted sounds of merrymaking issued from Custer's Last Stand. Traffic whooshed and rumbled by on Ponce de Leon two blocks away. A dog in the next block barked shrilly, starting a chorus of barking up and down the street.

"Dinah," said Clifford in a low voice, turning to her.

It was becoming an exciting kiss when the porch light flicked on and the door opened.

"Clifford!" gasped Aunt Charlotte.

Instead of springing apart guiltily, they unwound slowly and reluctantly from the embrace. Audacity supplied by alcohol, thought Dinah.

"Yes, what is it?" he said calmly.

After the involuntary outburst, Aunt Charlotte affected discreet imperception. "There's something or someone scratching at my window and looking in."

Clifford sighed. "All right. We'll go see what it is."

"It's probably Prince," said Dinah. "A Great Dane who lives directly behind us. The fence isn't high enough to keep him in, and he gets out and gambols about the neighborhood. He's very friendly."

Just as she had expected, she and Clifford found Prince standing on his hind legs looking in Aunt Charlotte's window. He saw them, and dropped to all fours and galloped toward them.

Clifford fell over a pile of handmade bricks Amanda was saving to build a terrace. Prince was all over him with frenzied affection, licking his face and making glad little snuffling and yipping noises.

Dinah bent to give him a hand. Clifford staggered to his feet and put his arms around her. Prince, incited by this friendly gesture, jumped up and embraced both of them, licking one face and then the other.

"Down, boy," she commanded.

"I thought you liked it," Clifford said in a hurt tone.

"I'm talking to Prince. There are too many in on this embrace." She shoved the dog down, patted his head, then put her arms around Clifford's neck again. "You may proceed."

He did.

Chapter Seven

Dinah awoke with all the disquieting symptoms of a hang-over—guilt, headache, dehydration, and the cringing paranoia manifested by the suspicion that somehow or other she'd made a fool of herself.

Feeling the urgent need of coffee, aspirin, and tomato juice, preferably by intravenous injection, she stood up, stumbled over a basket of clothes, and remembered she had been sleeping on the back porch.

She returned to the bed, rummaged about for her robe, and found it draped over the footboard. If only she didn't run into Clifford until she had ingested some healing remedies and also had a little time to gather her thoughts and decide how she felt about him. And there was a distressing recollection about David. She hadn't gone back to Custer's Last Stand, and didn't remember seeing David again after he went out to his car.

The confrontation with Clifford was not to be put off. Putting on her robe, she looked up to see him standing just inside the open kitchen door. He was regarding her with the warm combination of amusement and affection that only adorns the face of one who considers himself a lover, if not in the complete intimacy the word implies these days, at least in confident anticipation of it.

He, too, was wearing pajamas and robe. "My dear, you look lovely. How do you feel?"

"Rotten," said Dinah.

"A churlish attitude for one with whom I hope to share many breakfasts. But due to a hang-over, I trust."

She said irritably, "Are you always this cheerful in the morning?"

"No, no, purely an affectation, an overcompensation, you might say, for a disagreeable disposition. Actually," he confided in a lowered voice, "I feel pretty shaky too. Keeping up with your friends in the consumption of what Aunt Charlotte calls 'the drink' is ruinous to the health. Not to mention Ted and Aunt Amanda. My God, they must have started early in the afternoon."

"About twelve-thirty."

He held the kettle under the hot-water faucet. "Amazing how they can keep drinking so long and remain upright and coherent."

"Practice," she said.

"Coffee will bring the smile back to those rose-petal lips," he said confidently. "You do have instant coffee?"

"Oh, yes," she said absently, drifting over to the cabinet. "Also tomato and orange juice and aspirin."

"And scrambled eggs," he added.

Something that had been vaguely troubling her suddenly popped up into her conscious mind as she glanced at the clock. "Clifford, is Aunt Charlotte up?"

"I'd forgotten all about her. Getting more absent-minded every day. Must be some sort of mental feat to forget Aunt Charlotte. It's ten o'clock, and she isn't one to loll about in bed. I'll go look in her room."

He came back in half a minute. "Gone. But probably for a walk."

They ate in silence—the companionable silence, she thought, of people whose relationship had progressed beyond the necessity for small talk. She had only a hazy recollection of how this had come about and felt bewildered that it should be so. Clifford represented everything abhorrent to her. He had mentioned some of them yesterday. Rotary Club, right-wing Republicanism, and Junior Chamber of Commerce. Recalling the juvenile roistering of this last group during a recent convention in Atlanta, she put down her cup and shuddered.

"Clifford, do you belong to the Junior Chamber of Commerce?"

"I hope I'm not being insulting when I tell you it's very easy to read your mind, Dinah. To you, I'm a type, and a pretty repulsive one. Looking on the bright side, I hope it means you are attracted to me. Otherwise, I don't believe you'd bother about it for a minute." He put his hand on hers. "Are you?"

"Am I what?"

"Attracted to me."

"You know I am."

"Would it help your unease to tell you I don't like the Junior Chamber of Commerce and the Rotary Club, and that I'm not even a *liberal* Republican? I'm a C.P.A. and therefore not tied to my family's bank, but free to go into business for myself anywhere. I had been planning to leave and do that even before—even before I came down here."

"I'm very happy for you, Clifford. But how does this concern me?" (As if she didn't know.)

"You know perfectly well. Coyness doesn't become you,

Dinah. I know this will sound quaint and also precipitate, but what I have in mind is marriage. I'm sorry I can't ask you to live in sin with me, as they used to call it, but it just wouldn't do."

The corners of her mouth quirked. "Clifford, your intentions are insufferably honorable."

He grinned. "Ultimately. I certainly have no objection to getting better acquainted with you in the meantime. And I think something was said last night about a picnic. Picnics, as you know, I'm sure, offer rich opportunity for cementing friendships and all that sort of thing."

"Yes, I do know. And I remember we talked about it last night. But this morning I also remembered that I'm going on a picnic with David Winthrop."

He frowned. "That guy who was practically sitting in your lap last night?"

She said sweetly, "Speaking of practically sitting in people's laps, perhaps we could invite the glamorous Betty and make it a foursome."

"No thanks. I prefer to stay home and sulk."

Figuring that their relationship had progressed to the exchange-of-confidences stage, Dinah said, "Clifford, we were wondering why Aunt Charlotte suddenly decided to come down here and see us."

"I believe it has something to do with the faith healer she's taken up with."

"Faith healer!" gasped Dinah.

"You may well be astounded. We were. You should have seen my brother Hardin's face when he first heard of it. It clouded over like an El Greco landscape."

He took a sip of coffee and grinned at her. "You understand, of course, that Hardin's mental processes are operated entirely by greed. He was afraid Aunt Charlotte was going off her nut and might leave this guy something, or possibly everything.

"But at any rate," he went on, "he seems sincere about his healing powers. And the funny thing is that Aunt Charlotte's arthritis *is* a lot better. Mind over matter, I guess. Anyway, he believes in love. Hatred and bitterness and injustice release poisons in the body and must be replaced by love. If you drive all hatred from your heart and go about righting the wrongs you've done, you'll drive out the poisons that are making you sick."

"And you think Aunt Charlotte came down here to right the wrong she's done to Amanda?"

"Yes, I do. But as I say, she hasn't come out and told me anything. But on the way down here, she kept talking about this love stuff, and I got the idea she's planning to turn over Amanda's share, which should be half, she thinks. But since your grandfather invented the thing, I personally think Amanda should have all the bobbin rights."

"She personally thinks so, too," Dinah told him.

"I expect Aunt Charlotte will make a dramatic announcement at what she considers the proper time," said Clifford.

A rasping noise almost directly overhead cut into the ensuing silence.

"The doorbell," she told him.

In the hall, they were joined by Amanda, emerging from her room in an exotic Chinese embroidered robe, her uncombed hair looking more like a white chrysanthemum than usual.

"Who could be calling at the crack of dawn?" she asked hoarsely.

Amanda got there first and opened the door. Standing

on the threshold was a large blond man about forty in a dark blue suit.

Dinah was alarmed. He was Captain Mark Latham of the Atlanta police—of the Homicide Squad, to be precise. Although he was a friend who lived ten blocks away and his wife, Ivy, and sister, Beverly, were friends and fellow antique dealers of Amanda's, she was sure this was not a social call—even before she saw the uniformed policeman behind him.

Amanda, however, had no such apprehension. "My dear Mark, how good it is to see you. I was just talking to Ivy and Bev yesterday. We're planning to go to a country auction next week. Do come in."

Mark and the uniformed man came into the hall. Dinah was even more alarmed to see that Mark was a little discomforted by these effusions.

Amanda noticed the uniformed man at last. She said in a subdued voice, almost a whisper, "Mark, what is it?"

Chapter Eight

"We need to talk to you," said Mark soberly, looking around and adding, "Especially Mrs. Prentiss. Charlotte Prentiss, I think it is."

"Charlotte!" gasped Amanda. "What on earth has happened?"

"If you'll get Mrs. Prentiss, then I can tell you all at once."

Clifford said, "She isn't here."

"We don't know where she is," Dinah told him. "We think she must have gone for a walk."

"We need to find her right away," Mark said in a tone subtly different from what Dinah now thought of as his "friendly voice."

"Can't you tell us what this is about?" Amanda pleaded.

Mark countered with another question. "Do you know a man named Arthur Stockton?"

Amanda said bewilderedly, "No, I don't, and how could Charlotte know anybody here except us?"

"He's a biker—or was. One of the Desperadoes."

Amanda turned a stricken face to Dinah and Clifford. "That biker she was talking to last night . . ." She turned back to Mark. "Yes, Charlotte knows him—or knew him a long time ago. He used to be in her Sunday school class when he was a child. She ran into him on her way to the bar and they recognized each other."

Mark's face remained strangely impassive—eerily so, to Dinah, who was accustomed to seeing him as a friend with a dry sense of humor.

"When did any of you last see Mrs. Prentiss?"

Amanda turned to them. "I haven't seen her since she left the bar with you and Clifford, Dinah. I just assumed she was in bed asleep when I got home. She's in the room next to mine, and the door was closed."

"What about you, Dinah?"

"We took her home from the bar—oh, dear, that has an unfortunate sound. Aunt Charlotte doesn't drink. She knew Ted and Amanda were over there, at Custer's Last Stand, and when a fight broke out next door, she went over to tell them about it. That's when she ran into that Desperado. What I mean is that Clifford and I escorted her home. The fight next door was still going on, and the police arrived as we were crossing the street."

"That was the last time you saw her?"

"No, she—that is, Clifford and I were sitting in the porch swing, and Aunt Charlotte came to the door and said something or somebody was trying to get in her window. It was a Great Dane who lives behind us and jumps the fence. We went around to the window and Clifford shouted that it was the dog. She said something—I don't know what—and her light went out. That's the last time I saw her. It must have been about twelve-thirty."

Mark's inquiring glance shifted to Clifford. "I haven't seen her since then, either. But I wasn't worried. She gets up early. At home she goes for a walk every morning, and on Sunday, she goes to church. But I don't think it's likely she'd be at church since no one else was going and she's a stranger in the neighborhood."

"Did she eat breakfast?" asked Mark.

Clifford said, "If she did, she left no traces of it. But she wouldn't. She'd wash whatever she used and put it away."

Amanda cut in impatiently, "Tell us what has happened, Mark."

"Somebody found Arthur Stockton early this morning in the alley between Mimosa Way and Fern Terrace. His throat had been cut."

Amanda's hand went to her throat in an empathetic gesture of horror. "You can't think that Charlotte—I'll admit she has her crotchets, but she is almost obsessively law-abiding."

"We haven't formed any opinions yet," said Mark, in a voice that Dinah was sure he used just before warning people that they were entitled to get a lawyer. "We're just trying to talk to everybody who's seen him lately.

"But since nobody has seen Mrs. Charlotte Prentiss since last night—" He let the myriad implications hang in the air for a few seconds before going on. "I think you'd better look in her room, Amanda. See if she took off her night clothes and dressed after you last saw her."

"I'll go look, Captain," said Clifford. "Dinah, would you—?"

"Of course," she said stiffly.

In the guest room, they stood just inside the door, looking around at the Victorian bed neatly made up, the unoccupied look of the room except for the closed suitcase on a big old-fashioned trunk in front of the bed.

"How can you tell anything?" Clifford asked plaintively.

"If she weren't so neat—"

"I don't suppose you know what she brought with her,"

said Dinah, walking to the closet and opening the door on a black dress, the gray suit she'd worn yesterday, and a tailored robe hanging over a chaste cotton nightgown.

"She had on that robe last night. At least we know she got dressed. But in what?"

He shook his head. "I can guess what she might have brought. She has a green suit, and navy blue dress that she wears to church and parties. But she might have bought something new. I wouldn't necessarily know."

"Clifford, we've got to look for her."

"Yes, if that policeman— Surely, he's not detaining us, I believe they call it."

"How could he? We didn't know that biker. I've seen him around, of course. He's rather noticeable."

In the living room, Mark was sitting on a French chair, gingerly and on edge, as if he had lived with antique dealers and their wares long enough to gauge what chairs might or might not support his large frame. The uniformed man stood behind his chair.

Amanda was on the sofa, staring blindly at the mantel, for once bereft of the small talk which had carried her so smoothly through life.

Clifford said, "Her nightgown and robe are in the closet, so she dressed in something—I don't know what."

Captain Latham stood up. "She must have gone for a walk then. We'll look for her. Dinah, would you like to get dressed and come with us?"

Dinah nodded and Clifford said, "I'll go, too, if that's all right."

Dinah said, "I'll have to get my clothes out of the closet in the room where you're staying, Clifford."

In her room, she and Clifford stood in the closet door,

pulling out shirts and slacks—silently, as if, thought Dinah, anything they said would be a mistake.

She took her clothes to the big bathroom and dressed quickly, dashing water on her face and running a comb through her hair. But not thinking because the whole thing was so bizarre it was unthinkable.

Later she must ponder over Clifford's proposal, an odd thing for a sane man to do on such short acquaintance. Or reacquaintance, in this case. But their week together as teen-agers scarcely counted.

Clifford, looking somber and subdued, emerged from her room as she came out. He touched her hand briefly and turned to walk back to the living room. Neither of them had spoken since they left the living room to get dressed.

Chapter Nine

The search for Aunt Charlotte was conducted on foot, Mark and the patrolman walking behind Dinah and Clifford. The procession inspired a rumor that they had been taken into custody for questioning or possibly (and far more interestingly) arrested for the murder of Arthur Stockton.

Dinah felt a sinking, queasy feeling in the pit of her stomach when Mark directed them to go through the alley that ran past the winos' house on Mimosa Way and cut through to Fern Terrace beside one of the two houses occupied by the Desperadoes. Opening into it behind the bikers' houses was another alley that went through to Tarrant Place.

In between were the back yards of three houses facing on Rives Street. The houses had been recently restored or remodeled, turning the alley into a microcosm of the neighborhood's diversity.

Trash cans in the winos' back yard were surrounded by bottles once containing King Cotton wine and Polly Peachtree hair tonic, a local product whose printed warning that it was not to be taken internally was habitually ignored because of its high alcoholic content. Mingled with these were a couple of dozen bottles labeled Watkin's Internal Liniment, a product containing 48 per cent alcohol and presumably more roborant than Polly Peachtree.

The four averted their gaze from obscenities inscribed in white chalk on large portions of the basement wall and looked to the right at the miragelike incongruity of three town-house gardens with pebbled pathways and terra-cotta pagodas and Foo dogs sitting in immaculate beds of ivy.

At the other end of the alley, policemen milled around a tarpaulin spread on the ground. Dinah's stomach plummeted farther until she saw it was flat. The remains of Arthur Stockton had been removed to the morgue for the routine indignities.

The winos' back yard looked like something on the cover of *House and Garden* compared to the Desperadoes'. The big motorcycles were sprawled about on the ground amid the squalor of defunct refrigerators tilting like white towers of Pisa in a sea of mud and piles of discarded clothing, furniture, dishes, and bottles.

Mark stopped to talk to a plain-clothes man. Their uniformed escort joined the other policemen and Dinah and Clifford stood a little apart.

Mark joined them after a couple of minutes, and Dinah said, "It's so quiet here now."

"The rest of the gang has been taken in for questioning. Would you like to see the inside?"

"Well, yes and no. I confess to a sort of morbid curiosity."

"The morbidity grows as the curiosity diminishes," said Mark.

They walked in silence around to the front of the two houses—frame bungalows built in the depression when ostentation was out of favor with the wealthy and out of reach of everybody else. Product of an era when drabness was rampant, they were at least, before their sad comedown, a haven of lower middle-class respectability.

Mark walked ahead of them, pointing to a pitted substructure where a thick concrete step had been torn off its fieldstone base. "Wonder how they did that. Looks like it would take a hoisting crane."

All the windows along the front had been broken. Mark opened the screen door, also broken, and gave a mock bow to usher them into a scene of wreckage so complete that it looked like vandalism.

In what was once the living room, bare mattresses were flung about on the floor. The fieldstone fireplace was crammed with trash. The graffiti scrawled in black paint on the once-white walls achieved a marked virtuosity with the limited vocabulary of obscenity.

Dinah glanced at the piles of clothes on the floor. "I wonder if the clothes just accumulated or if each pile belongs to one person."

Mark laughed. "Maybe you can write an article on biker housekeeping, Dinah."

She shuddered. "God forbid. And if He didn't, Martin Sterling certainly would."

Clifford said, "Dinah, I don't want to seem overly fastidious about your neighborhood, but this place is getting on my nerves just a little."

"Had enough?" said Mark.

"Oh, yes," they assured him in unison.

On the porch, Mark said, "Where now?"

"Since this is Aunt Charlotte's first day in the neighborhood, we don't know where she might go for a walk," said Clifford.

"Well, first let's go around a couple of blocks—up Fern Terrace to Angola and back to Mimosa Way," suggested Mark.

They found Aunt Charlotte standing at the foot of the porch steps of a house on Mimosa Way a block from Dinah's. The house was near the top of the list of the Eyesore Committee, formed by the neighborhood association to do something about the worst first.

It was a big, two-story house afflicted with a particularly ugly siding that looked like brick-patterned linoleum of various non-brick shades of lavender, pink, green, and yellow.

The front porch was furnished with a living-room suite of tumescent overstuffed furniture covered with a scrambled brown and yellow upholstery which had long since given up and begun to spew out wads of stuffing.

A busy and often-angry colony of bees lived inside the partially disemboweled sofa, and it was the pastime of one of the drunks living in the house to sit on the sofa and try to catch them in his hands.

The sinking feeling which had become so familiar since yesterday hit Dinah again, for seated on the disreputable old sofa was a woman she knew only as Flo. An enormously fat woman whose mounds and hillocks of flesh, precariously contained in a size 44 slack suit, gave the appearance at first glance of someone sitting in the middle of a truckload of watermelon. Even in a neighborhood full of flamboyant drunks, she stood out.

She had been arrested on several occasions for being drunk and disorderly—a routine phrase which in no way conveyed the extent of her drunkenness and disorderliness since her particular idiosyncracy was disrobing on the porch or the sidewalk in order to gain the freedom of movement she felt necessary for practicing dance steps.

Although there was a Lotus-eaters' indifference to all sorts of bizarre goings-on among the Midtown populace, there were a few who felt that the sight of a nude Flo doing the Cha-Cha was too much of a good thing.

A couple of times, such was the exuberance of her spirits, she had also been charged with resisting arrest, another impoverished official term which fell far short of describing the actual spectacle of two young and embarrassed policemen grasping various portions of her person and calling plaintively for someone to bring a bedspread or tarpaulin to wrap around her.

Those who had witnessed one or both of the incidents reported that the policemen, by clutching her with widely encompassing arms and being more or less dragged along by a frolicsome and recalcitrant Flo, appeared to be joining in the dance.

Sitting on the sofa, a fifth of Heaven Hill and a bottle of Pepsi-Cola at her elbow, she was conversing with Aunt Charlotte, standing at the foot of the porch steps. The vast contours of her face looked amiable but puzzled.

"Clifford!" gasped Dinah.

Clifford, attuned by now to the neighborhood propensity for aberrant behavior, sprinted ahead of Mark and Dinah.

Drawing closer, Dinah heard Aunt Charlotte speaking in the imperious tones of a duchess visiting the tenantry. "How did you get so intoxicated on Sunday morning?"

Flo answered simply and truthfully, though somewhat slurredly, "Heaven Hill."

Aunt Charlotte, probably groping for some religious interpretation, appeared mystified until Flo waved a tree-trunk arm at the bottle beside her.

A bee emerged from a lump of exposed stuffing, and Flo swatted lazily at it.

Clifford walked up the concrete steps to the yard. "Aunt Charlotte," he said pleasantly, "we've been a little worried about you." And also pleasantly, he said to Flo, "Good morning."

Seismically animated by the sight of a good-looking man, Flo sat up and leaned forward, a move which shifted and rearranged vastitudes of flesh. "I was just asking your aunt to come up and have a drink with me, but she says she don't drink. How about you?"

Flo's features, located like Humpty Dumpty's somewhere near the center of the ovate, rippled and quivered with massive coquetry.

Clifford's stock with Dinah, already pretty high, soared into the stratosphere when he managed to keep a straight face and answer with solemn politeness, "Thanks a lot, but we've got to be getting home."

Aunt Charlotte, brought up as a small-town big shot and chock full of *noblesse oblige*, gave her a lofty smile. "I appreciate your hospitality, but I cannot help deploring your choice of pastimes, especially on Sunday morning."

Flo looked befuddled as she translated this into everyday language. Then her face shook and quivered, arranging itself into a tolerant smile. "Well, some like to drink and some don't, honey."

She hoisted her glass. "Here's to you, anyway."

On the sidewalk, Dinah introduced Mark as Captain Latham, leaving it to him to explain the title. He waited, however, till they reached the house.

"Mrs. Prentiss, I need to talk to you for a few minutes."

Aunt Charlotte stopped halfway up the steps. "What about?"

"I'll explain when we get inside."

Amanda and Ted stood up as they came in. Dinah's glance darted to the tray on the coffee table. The coffee mugs which had offended Ted yesterday would have been reassuring if she hadn't known of Ted's proclivity for adding alcohol to the most innocent of drinks—coffee, tea, lemonade—almost anything liquid and drinkable.

Amanda, in black slacks and turquoise knit shirt, hurried over to them. "Charlotte, we've been worried about you."

"I can't think why. I went for a walk, as is my custom every morning, arthritis permitting."

"But we thought—" Amanda's innate tact ran head on into the problem of telling her that her family thought she had been murdered because of her association with a biker. And, as usual in such situations, she chose a course of non-confrontation, or copping out, as Dinah phrased it.

She said to Mark, "Surely you told her about the biker."

Mark looked displeased. "Not yet. Suppose we all sit down."

"Yes, do sit down, and I'll bring some coffee," said Amanda.

As she left for the kitchen, Dinah marveled at her propensity for turning the grimmest gathering into a social occasion.

Aunt Charlotte, sitting in an Empire chair facing Mark—stuck again with the fragile French chair—immediately took charge. "Now, tell me what this is all about, Captain Latham. I assume you are a police officer and not an Army captain."

Dinah had never seen Mark visibly flustered before. But

probably he'd never questioned anyone like Aunt Charlotte before.

He smiled tightly and said, "As a matter of fact, I'm both—a captain in the Army Reserve and the Atlanta police department. But I'm here as a police officer today.

"I need to talk to you about Arthur Stockton, Mrs. Prentiss. I feel that you can give us some information because you knew him when he was a child and also talked to him last night."

"I'll be glad to help you in any way I can, but first tell me what has happened."

"He was found in an alley near here about five-thirty this morning. His throat was cut."

"Poor boy. I'm really not surprised, though. He told me he belonged to some sort of cycling club, but I was afraid he had fallen in with evil companions, Captain."

Mark's mouth twitched but his voice was solemn. "Why?"

"The things he said and the way he was dressed, in that black costume. There was something piratical about it. And then his background. I'm sure my nephew told you he was in my Sunday school class of boys in the mill workers' district of Andrewsville. The sort of environment which some overcome and some don't. He showed early signs of being one of those who don't."

"Like what?" said Mark, looking up with a slight frown at Amanda bearing a tray of coffee cups.

But she did not speak. She set the tray down on the massive Chinese Chippendale coffee table, and sat back down on the sofa.

"Stealing, habitual truancy, vandalism, attacking other boys. He'd been arrested two or three times before he was twelve. I gradually lost track of him. I concentrated on the ones who seemed salvageable. It may have been wrong."

"But understandable," said Mark. "Must have been about fourteen or fifteen years ago. He was twenty-six. He had probably changed a lot. How did you recognize him?"

"He recognized me. I'm sure I wouldn't have known him if he hadn't told me who he was."

Dinah wondered what Artie Stockton thought when he saw his redoubtable old Sunday school teacher. Of course he had recognized her. Aunt Charlotte had changed very little in fifteen years, being one of those people who adopts the dress and manner of middle age fairly early, so that they seem to reach a plateau in which the aging process stops for fifteen or twenty years.

"I was disturbed by the fight next door," said Aunt Charlotte.

"Fight?" asked Mark.

"Yes, yes," she said impatiently. "These boisterous young people—all fighting on the porch. The noise was unbelievable."

"I can believe it. So you decided to tell Amanda and get her to call the police."

"Yes, I'd heard them saying they were going to Custer's Last Stand and assumed it must be that place across the street. I hurried out the door and down the steps. I suppose I wasn't looking where I was going. I bumped into him on the sidewalk in front here. When I said, 'Excuse me,' or something like that, he looked at me and said, 'Miss Charlotte? You really are Miss Charlotte, ain't you?'

"Of course I recognized him when I looked closely at him. I said, 'Artie, what are you doing? Why are you wearing that ridiculous outfit?'

"He seemed flustered. He said, as near as I can recall,

'It's the uniform of a cycle club I belong to, Miss Charlotte.'

"I said, 'Are you still going to Sunday school and church, Artie?'"

Mark's face was having difficulty maintaining its impassivity. Ted made a choking sound. Dinah and Clifford exchanged glances.

"He said, 'No, not in a long time, but I still remember a lot of things you used to tell me.' Then he looked around as if he were making sure nobody was within earshot, and lowered his voice and said, 'Miss Charlotte, are you still my friend?'

"I assured him I was, and he said, 'I'd like to talk to you. There's something I need to ask you about.'

"I asked him, 'What about? What's the matter, Arthur?'

"He looked up and down the street as if he were making sure nobody could overhear. Although heaven knows, with that racket next door—

"Anyway, he then said, 'I'm in trouble, Miss Charlotte. I'm mixed up in something bad and I'm scared.'

"'Scared of what?' I asked.

"He lowered his voice almost to a whisper. 'Somebody's trying to kill me.'

"I thought perhaps I'd misunderstood him. It was hard to hear with all that racket. I said, 'Why, Artie? You must tell me.'

"He said, 'Because I . . . because I know too much. I know who—'

"And then he broke off as he looked up and down the street again. He said, 'I'll have to talk to you later. Can I come see you tomorrow morning, Miss Charlotte?'

"I told him of course. I insisted that he'd feel better if he told me then and probably I could advise him.

"But he said, 'No, tomorrow it'll have to be,' and started across the street.

"I got the distinct impression he didn't want to be seen with me inside the bar. As soon as we got inside the door, I said something about seeing him at ten in the morning and he mumbled something and walked over to the end of the bar, where he was still standing when we left."

Mark said, "Who did he see? Did someone drive up and get out of a car? Or maybe somebody came out of the bar or one of the houses near here."

Aunt Charlotte shook her head. "I'm sorry. I don't remember seeing anybody except those dreadful young people next door."

Mark stood up. "I'd appreciate it if you'd cast your mind back and try to remember someone who appeared suddenly on the street or sidewalk or in a car. If you think of it, please let me know immediately, Mrs. Prentiss."

Chapter Ten

Gilly Jones arrived as Mark was leaving. Her fragile-little-old-lady image included clothes. She was dressed primly in a navy skirt and chaste white blouse ornamented with a large cameo pin at the throat. Aunt Charlotte would think that here at last was someone respectable—until she opened her mouth.

Since Gilly lived across the street from the bikers in a charmingly remodeled yellow-brick apartment, she had probably seen and heard a lot and was anxious to tell it.

Aunt Charlotte bestowed a look of unqualified approval on her as Amanda introduced them. Dinah shuddered.

Amanda said, "Do have some coffee, Gilly, and tell us what's happening on Fern Terrace."

"My dear, the things going on over there call for a drink."

Dinah shuddered again as Amanda welcomed this idea with the enthusiasm of an alchemist whose lab partner has just made a gold ingot.

"I think we all need a drink. Ted."

The sound of the magic word roused Ted from glassy-eyed somnolence. "Oh, yes indeed. Splendid idea. Clifford, my boy would you like to help?"

When they had left, Amanda said, "I have another splendid idea. Gilly, why don't you stay for lunch. We're having a big bowl of shrimp and crab salad. Plenty for everybody."

"I accept eagerly and graciously," said Gilly. "Not to say hungrily. I was working all day yesterday and didn't get to the grocery store."

Gilly sat in the chair Mark had just left. Never one for beating around the bush she said, "What was Mark Latham doing here?"

Amanda beamed at her. "The strangest thing. That biker—Artie Stockton—you know, the one who was murdered—"

"Of course, I know," said Gilly tartly. "It happened only a stone's throw from my apartment."

"Well," Amanda went on, "he used to be in Charlotte's Sunday school class. She ran into him on her way to Custer's Last Stand last night and he recognized her and told her he wanted to talk to her."

"I know that, too," Gilly said proudly. "David Winthrop told me."

"How did he know?" asked Amanda.

"You and Ted told him. Don't you remember?"

"Of course," Amanda said huffily. "I just forgot it in all the excitement. And if you know so damned much, why are you asking all these stupid questions?"

"I asked only one question," Gilly pointed out. "I simply wanted to know what he was doing here."

Aunt Charlotte was staring at Gilly. "Are you Gillian Jones, the writer?"

Gilly gave her the look of simpering surprise almost universally affected by writers asked this question. "Well, yes, I'm *a* writer. One of many, you might say."

Amanda gasped. "Charlotte, have you read Gilly's books?"

Aunt Charlotte's face was turning ox-blood red. "I—ah—in the course of my work with wayward girls—"

Gilly gave a whoop. "Wayward girls. Man, that's quaint." She patted Charlotte's arm. "Things are different from when you and I were girls. Sex was just as popular then but nobody would admit it."

She went on in a reminiscent vein, "I remember when I was a girl, there was a long poem called *Diary of a French Stenographer*. And pretty racy stuff it was, too, even for these days. A copy of it was passed around at Miss Potter's School for Girls until one of the teachers took it away. Then it was passed around among the teachers until it fell apart."

Amanda glanced anxiously at Charlotte's flushed face. "Gilly, what about the murder?"

Gilly's delicate face brightened. "The commotion started about six this morning. You know Tim Dobson found him?"

"No," said Amanda. "Poor old soul. It must have almost sobered him up."

"I doubt it," said Gilly. "He was on his way home from a birthday party for one of his friends."

"At six in the morning?" asked Aunt Charlotte.

"No, around five-thirty. He lives at the other end of the alley on Mimosa Way. There was some delay in calling the police, I think. Nobody knows how long it took him to go home and tell the other winos about it and then go to the telephone booth across the street here. But it was six o'clock when the ambulance and police cars woke me up.

"They herded all the bikers into a paddy wagon and several police cars. I can't help wondering what's going to become of them. I'm writing a book about the counterculture, and I've been getting some material on the bikers."

"You've been interviewing them?" asked Aunt Charlotte.

"I talk to the girls—the Mamas they call them. I watch for times when the men leave the house and try not to let my revulsion show at what they tell me."

She lowered her voice. "My dear, their sex life is downright obscene. And you know I don't use that word loosely for just any run-of-the-mill orgies."

"Indeed not," said Amanda. Then desperately, "Gilly, could you autograph one of your books for Charlotte. I'm sure she'd love to have one."

"Oh, yes," said Aunt Charlotte.

"I'd love to, but I don't carry them around for casual visits to friends' houses."

"I have an extra one I bought at one of your autographing parties after you had given me one. I'll go get it."

Amanda stood up, and Dinah saw her indecision about whether to leave the room and risk more lewd revelations while she was gone.

Ted came in carrying a tray of drinks. Amanda, looking relieved at the sight of something that would keep Gilly's mouth occupied, hurried out of the room.

"Gilly, I'll serve you first," he said, stepping in front of her with the tray. "After all, the drinks were your idea. Clifford made it. That boy has a real flair for mixing drinks. This is vodka and orange and papaya juice. The bits of flotsam floating around are fresh pineapple. Loaded with vitamin C and other restoratives too numerous to mention."

"Beautiful," said Gilly, taking a sip, and then a gulp.

"Also delicious. And I can already feel the restoratives surging through my ancient arteries."

"Not at all," said Ted gallantly. "I mean your arteries are far from ancient. Lots of good mileage left in them."

He took off a glass for Aunt Charlotte. "Non-alcoholic for you, my dear."

"Thank you," said Charlotte, returning her wary but fascinated gaze to Gilly as if she were an X-rated movie she had wandered into by mistake.

Clifford and Amanda came back and Gilly was distracted from her shocking story by the pleasant task of autographing a book.

Aunt Charlotte stood up and said, "Thank you so much. I must go put it in my suitcase so I'll be sure to get it home safely."

After she had gone, Ted said, "I have an idea Charlotte is more worried about getting herself home safely."

"This visit has been eventful," said Clifford. "Dinah, I haven't had a chance to ask you about the fat lady Aunt Charlotte was talking to."

"She is the Lady Godiva of Mimosa Way—without the horse."

"You mean she—? No, you can't mean she goes around with no clothes on."

"Not all the time," Dinah told him. "Just occasionally."

"Flo?" asked Gilly. "My God, what was she doing talking to Flo?"

"Flo was sitting on the porch on that old sofa," she told Gilly. "I think she called to Aunt Charlotte as she walked past and asked her to come up and have a drink. Aunt Charlotte was giving her a lecture on temperance, particularly on Sunday morning, when we arrived."

To Clifford, she said, "Flo has a conviction, augmented

by Heaven Hill, that she must be free of clothing to do her dance steps. It's only when she does it in the front yard that neighbors call the police."

"An innocent pastime," declared Gilly. "Who, I ask you, does she harm? Nobody. She doesn't leave her own premises. She is neither mean nor vicious. Quite the contrary. And she provides entertainment for a number of people who are not blighted by puritanical views."

"Gilly, why do you run on this way?" Amanda said exasperatedly. "What if everybody went cavorting around naked?"

"But everybody doesn't. Do you think that if Flo were allowed to gambol about in the altogether unrestrained that it would start a mass disrobing? Of course not. Most people are far too inhibited, even on Mimosa Way. I say there is far too little merriment in the world, and those who provide it should be encouraged, not arrested."

Ted set down his glass and clapped. "Hear, hear. I agree with your basic premise," he said. "But I don't think it's puritanism so much as estheticism. It's her proportions that offend people's sensibilities."

"But it's the grotesquerie that makes it funny," Gilly argued. "If she were slender, it would just be vulgar."

"But I thought vulgarity is what you like," said Amanda.

Fearing that the two old friends were about to start one of their arguments, Dinah decided to switch to a safer subject. Although, she reflected wearily, there is no safe subject with Gilly. Being outrageous was her *modus operandi*, her stock-in-trade, her livelihood.

She said, "Gilly, we've had digressions from digressions since you started telling us about the murder."

Gilly took a sip of her drink and set it on the coffee

table. "Ah, yes. I ran out in my robe and pajamas and saw most of it. Police are still swarming around."

Amanda drew herself up and stared at Gilly, dawning comprehension on her face. "You told Mark about Charlotte and that biker," she accused.

"Yes, I did. And no harm done. He'd have found out some time today."

Dinah was surprised that the old sparring partners passed up this opportunity for a fight.

Amanda merely shook her head. "Yes, he would. It was a memorable scene with many witnesses."

Ted, who hated unpleasantness like Aunt Charlotte hated alcohol, went back to a less-controversial phase of the same topic. "Who could have done it?" he asked.

"Well, the neighbors say that they're drug pushers. Not just grass, but heroin."

"If you've been talking to the girls, it seems they would have told you things like that," he remarked.

Gilly took another sip and grimaced and set it down again. "They don't gab about stuff that could send them to prison. They enjoy telling me about their home life because I look so prissy and pretend it shocks me.

"They never mention crimes, even after I've read about it in the paper. Like the time a couple of months ago when a bunch of them was arrested in Alabama for mugging and robbing people at the stock car races. Somebody always puts up bail for them. The ranks were depleted that weekend, and then they came roaring back Monday night."

Aunt Charlotte came back, picked up her glass sitting beside Gilly's on the coffee table, and drank half of it before setting the glass down again.

Dinah said, "Have you been in the house, Gilly?"

"Not until this morning. I told Mark Latham I was writing about the bikers and he let me go through."

"Clifford and I saw the living room—if you could call it that. What did you think of it, Gilly?"

"It's a funny thing, but I believe it's had a salutary effect on my housekeeping. Housework, as you know, is foreign to my nature. But after seeing the ultimate of no housework at all I went home and washed two days' dishes and cleared a lot of mouldy stuff out of the refrigerator."

Amanda said solemnly, "Artie Stockton would probably be gratified to know he hadn't died in vain."

Before Gilly could think of a proper—or improper—retort, the telephone rang, and Amanda jumped up to answer it.

She came back smiling. "That was your boss, Miles Dennis. Martin Sterling is in town. He wants to bring him over and I invited them to lunch."

"What on?" Dinah said tactlessly. "I'm already having to add two big jars of stuffed olives for expansion."

"Put in more boiled eggs and mushrooms," said Amanda. "Grate some cheese in it. It's not the actual content of anything that counts. It's the spirit in which it's offered. What matters is hospitality, conviviality—"

"And booze," added Gilly. "Speaking of which, I think I'll go to the kitchen and add more of it to mine."

She looked down and saw that Aunt Charlotte's glass was empty. "How about you, Mrs. Prentiss? More fruit juice?"

Aunt Charlotte held out her glass. "Yes, thank you. It's very good."

To Dinah, she said, "Who is Martin Sterling?"

"He's the elderly multi-millionaire who owns the magazine I work on, *The Southern Conservationist*. He loves birds and wild animals and woodlands. An atonement, I suppose, for obliterating several thousand acres of woods with housing developments."

Gilly came back with two glasses and gave one to Aunt Charlotte. "I've never met Martin Sterling."

"Gilly, be careful what you say," Amanda warned. "Dinah likes her job."

"I'm always careful what I say."

"Yes, I suppose you are. Come to think of it, it would take considerable forethought to shock so many different people in so many different ways."

She jumped up as the phone rang again.

"Granny, I can't stretch that salad any more with what's here in this house," Dinah told her.

She shook her head and stood up. "I'll go back and get started on it. Try to find some more things to throw in it."

Clifford said, "May I help?"

She smiled warmly at him. "Yes, of course."

It occurred to her that their exit would leave only Ted to deflect Gilly's conversational bombshells, and she had the sneaking idea that he would encourage her.

Amanda came into the kitchen. "Oh, there you are, Dinah. That was David. I invited him to lunch. It's the least I could do after the shabby way you treated him last night. He waited around about an hour, talking to me and Ted. It was embarrassing."

Dinah felt her face getting hot—a manifestation of girlish chagrin which she thought she'd outgrown in high school.

"I'll explain to him about Prince frightening Aunt Charlotte."

"I don't believe you can convince him that he was

frightening her for a whole hour unless you plan to tell him he chased her up a tree."

Clifford made a strangled noise in his throat, and Dinah turned to give him a dirty look.

"This lunch," she said, "is going to be one of the highlights of the social season on Mimosa Way. Martin Sterling is such a courtly old Southern gentleman you never know when he's unhappy about something until he fires off a letter or memo about it. And even these are so flowery you have to read them twice to catch on that he's mad.

"The publicity about him always plays up the fact that he was a poor man who made it on his own. And it's true as far as it goes. But he was from a wealthy family who lost their money in the depression. And therefore not a truck driver in a tuxedo."

"I see no reason for such an elaborate warning," Amanda said haughtily. "No one is going to offend him. As a matter of fact, I believe I invited him and Miles Dennis last night, so it would have been a serious *faux pas* not to mention it today."

"Last night?" said Dinah with sharply rising inflection. "Where did you see him?"

"There's no need to get agitated. He came in the bar and stopped to chat. The meeting in the back was over by then, and Miles Dennis had joined us. I told him about Charlotte coming in with that biker, and he seemed amused. Then, in a burst of conviviality, so to speak, I probably invited them to lunch today."

"You must have been running amok with conviviality," said Dinah. "I've told you, Granny, that Sterling is very peculiar. That effusiveness covers a host of eccentricities and weird convictions that anybody is liable to run afoul of at any time. The best relationship is the least with a boss like that. And I hope to God he didn't catch on that you were drunk. He cherishes a lot of funny illusions about Southern ladies."

"Drunk! How can you say such a vile thing about a moderate drinker who had several glasses of sherry and a martini or two?"

Clifford sounded like he was choking again, and Dinah sighed. "Oh, never mind. It's all right. Maybe it's even a good idea. We've never invited him here before and it's time we did. If we're careful what we say—but there's Gilly. And Aunt Charlotte."

"Aunt Charlotte!" she repeated. "Amanda, I haven't had a chance to tell you what Clifford said."

"Clifford hasn't had a chance to hear what Clifford said, either," said Clifford. "Sometimes he blurts out things he'd rather not be quoted on."

"Oh, you know," said Dinah impatiently, "about Aunt Charlotte and the faith healer."

"Faith healer!" exclaimed Amanda.

"Yes, he says she's taken up with a faith healer who believes in love—"

"Love! You mean Charlotte and this faith healer—"

"No, not that kind of love, Granny. The love of humankind. He has convinced her that rancor and hatred and injustice release poisons in the body, and you must get rid of all that kind of stuff to get rid of the pain. Of arthritis, in her case."

Amanda's stunned glance shifted from one to the other. "So you think she's come down here to turn over the bobbin rights to me?"

"Yes, I do," said Clifford. "Or part of it, anyway, although she hasn't said so. But she wouldn't confide in me.

She still thinks of me as a potentially delinquent schoolboy."

"And she's waiting for the proper time to announce it," mused Amanda.

"I'm sure of it," Clifford told her.

"But don't start hinting, Granny," Dinah warned. "You might get her back up and make her change her mind."

"We'd better get started on the salad," Clifford sensibly suggested.

Amanda headed for the door. "I'm going back to my duties as moderator. They'll be here any minute."

"Sufficient unto the day is the evil thereof, and all that," Clifford soothed sententiously, putting his arms around Dinah.

"This is about the evilest day I can remember. It should be spread out over a couple of years."

"But think what a big chunk of evil you're dispensing with all at once," he said. "Things aren't very pleasant with Aunt Charlotte here, anyway. So why not combine your difficulties?"

"Clifford, what a genius you have for making unbearable things sound jolly."

"I want you to realize what a sunny little fellow I am and how necessary I am for your happiness and well-being."

Dinah laughed and kissed him on the cheek. "Sunny you may be, but little you are not."

She moved over to the refrigerator and started pulling out packages of vegetables—lettuce, mushrooms, cauliflower, spinach, celery.

"You're planning to chop up all this produce?"

"We certainly can't serve it like this," she told him. "So

let's get chopping. Oh, and eggs. We mustn't forget to boil a lot of eggs."

"Which will have to be chopped," said Clifford gloomily.

Ten minutes later, the Empire table's black marble top was piled high with vegetables chopped and unchopped.

Amanda hurried in looking wide-eyed and distressed.

"Charlotte is drunk," she announced.

Chapter Eleven

Clifford looked up from the cauliflower he was chopping. "She couldn't be. Never had a drink in her life—or so she says, and I've never doubted it."

Ted came in chuckling but stopped when Amanda glared at him. Casting a beaming glance around the room, he looked, thought Dinah, even more than usual like one of P. G. Wodehouse's potty old peers.

"How did she get drunk?" asked Dinah.

"Gilly!" Amanda's voice shook with rage. "She'll do anything to start trouble. 'Churning up catalysts', she calls it. I should have caught on. She switched glasses. It was easy to do. Her glass was beside Charlotte's on the coffee table. Then after Charlotte drank that, she brought her another from the kitchen."

"What a wicked old woman," Ted exclaimed admiringly. "How I envy her gall. She does the things everybody else wishes they had the nerve to do. Frankly, Amanda, I used to think she was a strange sort of friend for you. But, by God, she can add sparkle to the dullest gathering."

"This gathering wasn't exactly dull to begin with," said

Dinah. "More like a bartenders' picnic in the Baptist parking lot."

Clifford pushed back his chair and stood up. "We'd better go see about her. Gilly might be giving her more vodka."

"Oh, yes, she would," said Amanda. "Will," she corrected herself, hurrying through the door.

Ted stayed in the kitchen to make himself a drink. Dinah and Clifford followed Amanda.

Aunt Charlotte was a disheartening sight. Her normally erect figure was draped loosely over the chair, one foot on the coffee table. She was leaning toward Gilly, regarding her with owlish fascination.

"Tell me more about how you gather material for your books, Miss Jones. Do you actually witness these debaush—goings-on?"

"Sometimes," said Gilly. "In the one about prostitutes—You remember that one?"

"Oh, yes. Shertainly. Certainly."

"Well, I took this screen with me—a folding screen with Chinese scrolls on it—"

"Aunt Charlotte, let me get you some coffee," Clifford cut in.

"And a sandwich," added Dinah.

She waved them away with a flap of her hand. "Later. I'm talking to Miss Jones. You see I'm talking to Miss Jones, Clifford. So get lost."

Dinah was pleased to see that Clifford's aplomb could be shaken.

Heavy footsteps on the porch ended her smugness.

Amanda opened the door. It was David. Dear God, she'd forgotten about David. How could she explain her dereliction last night in front of all these people? Or even alone with him?

She went to him. "David, we're so glad you could come. I think you know everybody—except Aunt Charlotte."

She raised her voice as if she were shouting into an ear trumpet. "Aunt Charlotte, this is David Winthrop, Ted's nephew."

"How do you do?" She made it sound like an actual question.

David was puzzled, obviously suspecting the truth but not quite believing it. "How do you do, Mrs. Prentiss."

"Oh, very well, most of the time, thank you, except for occasional bouts of arthritis."

"I'm sorry to hear that." He was looking more and more uncomfortable.

She flapped her hand. "It's nothing. Comes and goes. Here today, gone tomorrow."

"Speaking of here today, gone tomorrow, what have you heard about the murder?" Dinah asked brightly.

"I didn't hear about it until I got up and out of the house a little while ago. I slept late."

He was proceeding guardedly, ready to be amenable to an acceptable explanation for being stood up or angry at a flimsy one.

Hoping to get him alone for a couple of minutes, Dinah said, "Ted's in the kitchen. Come on back and get a drink."

She carefully averted her gaze from Clifford, but he stayed in the living room—the absolute embodiment of tact. She was growing fonder of him by the minute. David, by contrast, seemed surly and difficult. She sloughed over the fact that he had every reason to be surly and difficult.

In the hall outside the kitchen door, she said, "I can't tell you how sorry I am about not being able to get back over last night, David, dear. First there was the fight next door. The police came and took away all the Grass Menagerie. Then after Aunt Charlotte calmed down and got to bed she was frightened by a Great Dane trying to get in her window. I didn't even think to call you because—well, to tell the truth, I'd had a good bit to drink."

He smiled—a very nice smile which lighted the blue eyes. "All is forgiven. And I suppose lunch will have to be a substitute for our picnic."

"I'm afraid so. I wasn't the only one who had too much to drink. Amanda was issuing invitations to lunch like Buckingham Palace, and she forgot all about it. We're having quite a crowd. Martin Sterling and Miles Dennis are yet to arrive."

He shook his head. "Quite a crowd in more ways than one. And your aunt seems a little under the weather."

"Gilly switched glasses with her. Aunt Charlotte's never had a drink before."

"So you have no precedent to predict her behavior. And your big boss and little boss on the way here. Poor Dinah."

She pushed open the kitchen door. "Not too much sympathy, please. I might bust out crying."

Ted looked up from his full-time avocation of mixing drinks. "Ah, there you are, my beamish boy. Thought you'd be rushing over to find out about the excitement after I called you early this morning. I got over there quick. Heard the sirens."

David said, "I went back to sleep after you called. Saloonkeepers stay up late on Saturday night."

"And I don't presume to mix drinks for saloonkeepers," said Ted. "Be your own bartender."

Dinah said, "I must go on with the chopping."

David offered to help, and she could think of no good

reason to refuse, since she couldn't very well tell him that Clifford had been her chopping date.

But Clifford, damn him, with his serene self-confidence, seemed not at all jealous. He behaved as if it were foregone that she would forsake all others. And if David happened to be one of the others, he wouldn't be around long.

She longed for a quiet moment to reflect on her feelings about Clifford. Their affair was hurtling along with cinematic celerity. She had learned from a lot of observation and a little experience that whirlwind affairs often died down as suddenly as they had begun.

One of the few gems of grandmotherly advice from Amanda had been, "Always have a backup. You wouldn't think of going through life with only one friend. So don't let one man monopolize you. When you get so far gone on a man you start breaking engagements and skipping meetings to be with him, one night you'll find yourself sitting at home alone because it's about six months too late to call your friends."

Sensible, though cynical advice. And after her parents had been killed in an automobile accident when she was nine, grandmotherly advice was about the only kind she had. Yet most of it was pretty sound. Amanda's flightiness was partly a pose affected by a lot of Southern women who grew up during an era when shrewdness was unladylike.

She simply had no way of knowing yet whether Clifford was one of these people who falls in love often and desperately and gets bored when he's sure of somebody.

David, chopping celery, said quietly, "Dinah, I was about to offer you a penny for your thoughts but they must be worth more than that for sheer weight."

"Oh, sorry. This has all been pretty distracting."

She turned to Ted, still fussing with drinks, "You missed out on some of the fun. I suppose Amanda told you about our little interlude of thinking maybe Aunt Charlotte had been murdered, too."

"Ah, well," said Ted, "I've reached the age where one must make judicious choices about how much fun he's able to take."

David said, "I had gone to my car, and I saw her coming in with that biker."

"And what a sight it was," said Ted. "Many of your patrons are peculiarly sensitive to such a phenomenon. The fact that everybody else saw it is no comfort, for everybody else is also hovering on the brink of hallucination."

David said, "Do you think she might have talked to him later?"

"I don't see how," said Dinah. "She says not, and I doubt if she'd lie about a thing like that, or about anything. She went home and went to bed. She'd have to dress again and sneak out of the house. No, she wouldn't have. She had arranged for him to come see her this morning."

"It's probably a good thing she didn't," said David. "Whoever killed him might think he'd told her something."

"Who could have killed him, David?" asked Dinah.

He shrugged. "I imagine there's a wide choice. He led a violent life. You know they're drug pushers?"

"Yes, I'd heard. It could be somebody he'd started on drugs, or even a relative of one of his victims."

"Or a relative or lover of one of the girls who lives there," David speculated. "Whatever background they came from, it had to be more respectable than that."

Ted drifted out carrying a couple of drinks, then hurried back. "Gilly and Amanda are having a fight in the hall."

"It doesn't matter," Dinah said. "With Aunt Charlotte smashed, we can relax and be ourselves—until Martin Sterling gets here."

The buzzer rasped. "Right on cue," she said, jumping up, rushing through the door, then slowing to a sedate walk in the hall.

Gilly and Amanda faced each other outside the kitchen door. Amanda was saying heatedly, "If it had been the first time, Gilly—your childish practical jokes. But no. Putting a whoopee pillow under the cushion in dear old Dr. Burdin's chair. And that nice young minister you brought here—slipping a package of contraceptives in his pocket so that when he pulled out his handkerchief—"

She drew breath for a fresh onslaught. "Nobody but you has seen a whoopee pillow since 1935. Your jokes are just plain tacky."

She had chosen a word that set Gilly off like a roman candle. "Tacky!" she shrieked. "Tacky!"

Dinah stepped between them. "Break it up, do you hear. You invited Martin Sterling here and you're going to help me do something about this Mad Tea Party. Go in there quick and see if you can get Aunt Charlotte out of there."

Her cold calm anger impressed Amanda. "All right. Come on, Gilly, and help undo some of the damage you've done."

Passing the living room archway, Dinah took it all in in an anxious glance. She wouldn't put it past Ted to give Aunt Charlotte more vodka. She gave Clifford a tight-lipped smile.

Aunt Charlotte's foot was still on the coffee table. She

stared into her empty glass as if she were beginning to suspect it might explain the enigma of the unprecedented way she was feeling.

Through the plate glass in the front door, Dinah beamed a fake smile at Miles Dennis and the tall, white-haired and imposing man beside him.

Martin Sterling looked like a multi-millionaire even in what the men's magazines call "casual clothes." His knit shirt and gray slacks had cost a lot of money. But even in shabby clothes, he'd still look rich. In his gray eyes was the combination of arrogance and benevolence seen only in very self-assured people.

She opened the door. "Miles. Mr. Sterling. I'm glad to see you." She marveled that she could make these social sounds under such trying circumstances.

She watched Aunt Charlotte during the little flurry set in motion by new arrivals—introductions, offers of drinks, seating. She tried to convince herself that a casual observer might not catch on that Aunt Charlotte was drunk—and, to her dismay, failed.

Miles already knew. He gave her a wicked grin which parted his beard in a display of large white teeth. Whatever happened, she was sure to be mercilessly kidded about it for a week.

Amanda offered them a choice of tea, coffee, or vodka and fruit juice. They wanted vodka.

"Wine is a mocker; strong drink is raging," Aunt Charlotte announced bibulously.

As a conversational gambit, thought Dinah, it left much to be desired.

Sterling regarded her uneasily. "You disapprove of drinking, Mrs. Prentiss?"

"Absho—absolutely. Never had a drink in my life." She

turned to face him for this pronouncement, and her foot fell off the coffee table, hitting the rug-covered floor with a loud thunk.

Gilly snickered. Amanda shot her an angry glance. "Would you care for a drink, Gillian?" she said with exaggerated sweetness.

Gillian inadvertently eased the tension she had created simply by being who she was.

Sterling said, "You must be Gillian Jones, the writer. Miles said you lived near here, and I told him I wanted to meet you."

Amanda said, "I'm surprised you didn't meet her at the bar last night. She's always in the bar on Saturday night. But maybe she went home before you got there."

Gilly, open-mouthed but silent, was obviously torn between reminding her friend that she, too, was a regular patron of the bar and making a favorable impression on a new admirer. She chose the latter, and kept quiet.

Amanda went to the kitchen. Dinah decided to follow as soon as politely possible. She longed to escape. And must escape to finish the new gigantic salad so this frolic would eventually come to an end.

She was thankful for Sterling's interest in urban problems and the restoration of the inner city. She relaxed a little while he talked with Gilly about her books.

Then she began to notice that he looked uncomfortable. And no wonder. Aunt Charlotte was staring at him with the unnerving fixity of alcoholic concentration. Clifford saw it, too, but after all, he was sitting across the room. And what could anyone do?

Then she spoke. "Dinah, I thought you said he was old. He looks pretty spry to me. Damn well preserved."

"Just a manner of speaking," said Dinah with a tinny

laugh. "I say old about the people I'm fond of—old Ted, old Clifford, old Miles."

"And old acquaintance be forgot," added Miles, who was enjoying himself hugely.

"I do the same thing," said Sterling, giving her the serene smile of unshakeable self-esteem.

She stood up. "I must go see about lunch."

This time Clifford and David and Amanda pitched in, all chopping at top speed while she hurried back and forth setting the dining room table for a buffet.

The murder provided a diverting lunch topic. Ted and Gilly gave their near eye-witness accounts. Amanda told about Mark Latham's visit. Like most frightful experiences, Dinah reflected in a mellow mood, it was already becoming a lively conversation piece. No doubt it would improve with the embellishments of time.

She and Clifford had brought in dining-room chairs and set them in a semi-circle in the dining-room archway. She had hoped to break up the pre-lunch seating arrangements, to separate Sterling from Aunt Charlotte. But Clifford had an even better idea. Fearing that Aunt Charlotte was too drunk to get around the dining table, he brought her a plate and persuaded her to sit on the sofa—in the hope, he confided to Dinah, that she'd go to sleep after lunch.

And so she did, after eating about a third of her salad and taking a couple of sips of coffee. Her head lolled back against the sofa. She pulled a crocheted antimacassar over her face, where it rose and fell like a tent flap as she began to snore.

From then on, it was a lovely party to Dinah. The rest of the afternoon had a dreamlike quality, perhaps because she too was sleepy.

Sitting in one of the dining-room chairs between Miles and Clifford, she was kept awake mostly by the uncompromisingly upright position in the straight-backed chair.

Martin Sterling said, "Your neighborhood is interesting. To think of the variety of people living here. I've never seen a place with so many strata of society. And no doubt that's why you live here, Miss Jones. Or is it Mrs.?"

"It used to be Mrs., but I was divorced such a long time ago that most people don't know I've ever been married."

Looking at Gilly's aristocratic old face, Dinah thought that though she was a bit trying at times she was never dull. She was reputed to have had several flamboyant affairs, one with a Methodist bishop. Although Dinah suspected the bishop story might be apocryphal, it was so typical of Gilly that if it wasn't true, its likelihood had prompted someone to invent it.

"I live lots of places for short periods collecting material," said Gilly, "but I keep my apartment here. I even lived in the suburbs for ten months. I rented a house on a dead-end street. The house was for rent because the owner had died of a heart attack, and his widow decided to live with her sister for a year or so before she made up her mind whether to sell it.

"Of course, she did sell it. The suburbs do not take kindly to single people, especially an oddball like me. And they thought I was very odd indeed. Not for the many sound reasons you might think, but because when I'm working in the morning, I don't get dressed till eleven or twelve. And a housewife who goes to the door in pajamas and robe at eleven in the morning is considered a slattern, or worse.

"On that short dead-end street there were ten houses,"

she went on in a declamatory voice. "In about a year and a half, five men—heads of families as we are wont to call them—had dropped out in one way or another. Four died of strokes or heart attacks and the other ran away—disappeared. It's a terrible setup. The men are kept on a treadmill and die of stress. The women are buried alive and die of boredom."

Ted said, "I, too, lived in the suburbs, Gilly. The kind you're talking about. There are suburbs for the old rich and the new rich and the merely prosperous. The old rich have a certain flair and style; money has settled gracefully on them like lichen on old gravestones. The new rich are amusing in a pathetic sort of way. But I lived among the merely prosperous, and they're the dullest, the most homogenized.

"I kept looking at my astro-turf lawn surrounded by acres of more astro-turf lawn, and I hated it. So I had it dug up and planted with zinnias, princess feathers, and marigolds with a few tomato and cabbage plants thrown in to give a nice rural effect."

He gave a chuckle reminiscent of Lord Emsworth on one of his pottier days. "My neighbors did not appreciate it. Most of them came from rural places, and I suspect my yard was too poignant a reminder of the old homesteads.

"They came to me in a body, or several bodies; one or two still fairly shapely but most grown paunchy from easy living. They told me my yard was ruining the looks of the whole street. I told them that perfection needs imperfection for comparison, that my yard enhanced the looks of theirs. They left—just sort of backed out the door and went home. And I never heard any more about it."

Gilly laughed. "Bully for you. I'm afraid I didn't stir up things in my little dead end of suburbia. It was stupefying.

All the time and energy wasted on the pretense of wholesome living."

She rounded on Martin Sterling. "But you, sir, have blighted the landscape with vast tracts of ticky-tackies. I find your interest in our neighborhood most disquieting."

Sterling leaned toward her, eager for the fray. "Yes, but no more. They say we profit from our mistakes. And I've made enormous profits from mine. If you've made a lot of money out of your transgressions, you can afford to rectify them, at least partially.

"No, Miss Gilly, I wouldn't tear down your old houses and apartments. I'd mostly just fix them up, as you've been doing, and maybe add a few new apartments and one or two condominiums."

David regarded him with a realtor's gleam in his eye. "Sir, are you interested in buying property here?"

"Yes, indeed. I'd like to start out on a small scale. Say a house for myself and an apartment to play around with. I've come around to the idea that you must live in a place for a while before you start making drastic changes."

Dinah was jolted awake by a blinding flash of inspiration. "What about the bikers' houses, Mr. Sterling. You'd have to see them to appreciate what a challenge they'd be."

"Are they for sale?"

"I'm sure they will be," said Gilly, her wanton old face lighting up in a Machiavellian smile. "Everybody wants to get rid of them. But the problem has been that everybody's afraid of them. Mr. Margolius, the housing code inspector for this section, says frankly that he's afraid to go in there. But now that they're out and in jail, we plan to get him over to inspect the houses and condemn them.

"The police have locked up the houses and don't intend

to let anybody in there until they finish with them. But they'll let Mr. Margolius in to inspect them. After they're condemned, nobody can live in them."

"What happens to condemned houses?" asked Sterling.

He had only been asking questions, but Dinah was sure he was hooked. The houses represented a whole bunch of obstacles to a man who loved obstacles. He had found that obstacles disappear as money accumulates, and the rich man is forced to create them.

David said, "I know the woman who owns them."

Amanda said, "I thought it was a couple."

David grinned. "It was. But they got a divorce and she got the two houses."

"Do you think she'll sell?"

"I imagine so," David told him. "I can call her."

Gilly, having correctly assessed Sterling's need for difficulties, enlarged on the theme in a throbbing voice. "Think of it! Creating beauty from all that ugliness. I'd love to do it myself if I had the money."

Knowing quite well that she did have the money and would no more think of buying those houses than joining the Women's Christian Temperance Union, Dinah was afraid she might be overdoing it.

But Sterling, with his vast sums of money, had completely lost sight of what could be done with lesser amounts. To him, Gilly was several notches below the poverty level. Still he was no fool. So he went back to the question no one seemed to have heard. "What happens to condemned houses?"

"Well, in this case, it will be a good thing," Gilly told him. "Nobody can live in them until they're fixed up to meet the housing code. So the woman who owns them could fix them up herself or sell them as is and the new owner would have to do it."

Sterling pondered this for a few seconds while the others sat with drawn breath, except for Aunt Charlotte, who continued to snore.

"I'd like to see them tomorrow morning, if it can be arranged." He spoke with the assurance of one who knows that anything he suggests can and will be arranged.

"I can arrange it," said David, carefully keeping out of his voice any suggestion of the dismay he must be feeling at the thought of all the tearing around and telephoning on a Sunday evening. "No trouble."

Chapter Twelve

The guests all acted as if they were settling in for the night, but somehow they cleared out by five o'clock.

Miles cornered Dinah in the kitchen and gave her his wry, whiskery smile. "My dear, your party was a rollicking success. Aunt Charlotte is more fun than a barrel of monkeys; Gilly was in rare form; and you made the coup of the year getting Martin interested in buying property in this neighborhood. You are in the class with those developers who sold all that underwater land off the coast of Florida."

"Cut it out," she said ungraciously, and then softened this crudity with a smile and asked, "What with one thing and another, I was wondering if I could have the day off tomorrow."

He considered for only a couple of seconds. "What with one thing and another, I suppose you may. But don't forget to come in on Tuesday."

"Oh, gee, thanks. You are one boss in a million. You are bossdom's Thane of Cawder, Wizard of Oz, Crack of Dawn."

"Cut it out," said Miles gruffly.

David and Martin Sterling exchanged telephone

numbers as they got up to leave. Aunt Charlotte snored on under the flapping antimacassar.

When they had all gone, Clifford leaned over Aunt Charlotte and shook her gently. "Come on, Aunt Charlotte. The clock in the steeple strikes five, and you'll be more comfortable in your bed."

"Oh, let her alone," said Amanda. "She's going to have one hell of a hang-over when she wakes up. The longer she sleeps, the better she'll feel."

Dinah said, "When the voice of experience speaks, others heed."

"The voice of experience needs a nice long rest," Amanda told her. "I'm going to take a nap, and I don't want to be awakened unless the house is on fire."

She went to her room and shut the door.

Clifford sighed. "I wanted to sit with you on the sofa, love, but Aunt Charlotte makes it an uncomfortable threesome."

He glanced apprehensively at the antimacassar rising and then falling to fit snugly over her face until the next snort blew it out again.

"You don't suppose there's any danger of her smothering under that thing?"

"Oh, no," Dinah assured him. "Even if she stopped snoring and it stayed over her face, it's a loose pattern with good-sized holes."

"Then, we'll just leave it there. It might wake her up if we take it off, and I don't want to wake her up. But that racket is not an appropriate accompaniment to what I had in mind."

"What did you have in mind?"

"Courting, I think it used to be called."

She grinned. "But not any more. If that's all you have in mind, we can sit on that day bed on the back porch."

"I always feel that plans should be kept flexible," he said solemnly. "We might have more privacy in your apartment on one of those window-seat arrangements turned over so hospitably to an unexpected and uninvited guest."

"Uninvited, maybe, but welcome," said Dinah, matching the solemnity in his voice. "And becoming more so by the hour."

At the door of her apartment, Clifford bowed. "Won't you come into your parlor . . ."

Dinah woke up in darkness and confusion about where she was, what day it was, what time it was, and who the man was beside her. She identified her room first, by the shapes and location of furniture, and then Clifford.

The time was more elusive. It could be early evening, late evening, or early morning. If it was the last, Aunt Charlotte would be shocked and even Amanda would be displeased.

"Clifford," she whispered.

He turned over, then sat up and yawned. "What time is it?"

"I was just wondering. If it's early morning, I'll have to sneak out quick to my bed on the back porch."

"I'm afraid so. Or Aunt Charlotte will make a public announcement that you are not eligible to wear white at our wedding."

"Clifford, I don't like big weddings. Neither does Amanda."

He yawned. "Fine. That makes three of us. How about some coffee?"

"It's one of the few things I have back here in this little kitchen."

She stood up. "Clifford, do our clothes look slept in?"

"Not at all. A triumph for modern fabrics. 'If you must keep your clothes on to sleep with your girl, try our new polygamous fibers. No crease, no crush, no crumple.'"

Dinah walked over to look at the electric clock on her chest of drawers. "Nine o'clock. A respectable hour. And, as you have just pointed out, we are decently and unrumpledly clothed. So if you'll straighten out that spread while I put the water on . . ."

"I like that word 'unrumpledly.' See if you can say it again."

"After I have coffee," she told him. "If we get any static from Aunt Charlotte about being sequestered back here, we can remind her that we couldn't sit in the parlor like a proper courting couple because she was passed out on the sofa."

He stood up. "I ought to go see about her, but I need coffee before I can face the sight of Aunt Charlotte with a hang-over."

He opened the small refrigerator to get out a carton of milk. "My God, how you've corrupted us, Dinah."

"Oh, Clifford, you should have seen you and Aunt Charlotte getting out of that Cadillac and looking around. And when those boys threw the firecrackers in the yard—" she was overcome by a seizure of giggling.

"Funny, eh?" he said grumpily. "We were decent folk until we got to this slough of iniquity. Aunt Charlotte had never had a drink in her life. Not to mention being mixed up in the murder of a biker."

"Next you're going to tell me you were a virgin and I lured you to my bed."

He set down the milk carton and put his hands on her shoulders. "No, love. But Aunt Charlotte might see it that way. So it's vital that you make an honest man of me."

"Oh, Clifford," she said fondly, "you really are absurd. And to think I wrote you off as a total loss ten years ago."

"You were a very foolish girl," he said sternly. "And you were about to write me off again when I first got here."

Her hand went to his cheek. "No, darling. You know what I thought when you came in the kitchen yesterday in your gray slacks and navy blue shirt?"

"No, what?"

"I thought 'wow!' And then as your personality began to unfold, as it were, I decided you were a winner."

He smoothed back her hair and kissed her forehead. "And what did you think a while ago?"

"I went back to 'wow!'"

"Oh, darling," said Clifford, and proceeded to kiss her expertly and fervently.

After a couple of minutes of this sort of thing, Dinah reluctantly pulled away to take the noisily boiling water off the stove.

Sitting beside her on one of the window-seat beds, he said, "Listen, Dinah, after Aunt Charlotte wakes up and gets over what will probably be a wing-ding of a hangover, I'm going to tell her that I'll go back with her just to take her home, pack my stuff, and tell my brothers I'm leaving. Then I'm coming back here, and we'll look for a house near here."

"Clifford," she began doubtfully, "I don't think—well, this is such a drastic change from your life in Andrewsville."

"Believe me, darling, I've been looking for the most drastic change I could find, and this is it."

Dinah was still troubled. "It sure is."

"And you are the most drastic—not to say delightful—change from the girls in Andrewsville. I doubt if you've ever known any girls like that. Southern Belles all of them. They're like the alligator gar. You look at them and think, 'My God, these creatures have got to be extinct.' But there they are, alive and breathing.

"Some of them may have been smart to begin with. It's hard to tell because they've all done this brain surgery on themselves—a do-it-yourself lobotomy. They sit around talking about social functions and what everybody was wearing and who went with whom.

"Every now and then I ask one of them, 'Sally Dale or Mary John, what are you planning to do?' She'll look at me in great wonderment and say, 'Do? Ah don't know what you mean, Cliffawd.'

"Then I say, 'I mean what kind of work are you planning to do?' And they look shocked and say, 'Why, Cliffawd, you know Daddy doesn't want me to work.'

"And then they move out of Daddy's house into John Bell's or Will Junior's house and they don't do another thing worth mentioning, unless you count occasionally giving birth in a genteel, unobtrusive way."

"But think how well they go with the men," said Dinah.

"Oh, yes. The women are passively dull; the men are aggressively dull. Can you imagine spending a whole morning on a golf course with a guy who inherited his father's appliance store or one who inherited his uncle's bank.

"I am speaking now of my brother Hardin. He and his wife, Betty Sue, are the dullest damn people you'll ever meet. Everything they say sounds like it came out of a book of conversations for Southern ladies and gentlemen.

There's the conversation about the golf tournament on page 235, and the one about the steeple chase on page 346. The real sparkler is the golf tournament that got rained out."

Dinah set down her cup and kissed him on the cheek. "Poor Clifford. But how do you know I won't get like that?"

He eyed her suspiciously. "No, you couldn't. Could you?" he asked plaintively.

"Well, I was hoping to snag a rich man or one of modest affluence, at least, so I can quit working—"

He gripped her elbows. "And get like Betty Sue?"

"No, Clifford, because I want to write novels. As a matter of fact, I've already written one. I took it to Gilly's editor in New York a couple of months ago, and he said, 'This is not good enough. But the next one will be. So start writing it.'"

He gave a gusty sigh and leaned back against the cushions. "I knew you were putting me on. If I were to wake up some morning ten or fifteen years from now, and it dawned on me that you'd turned into another Betty Sue . . ." He shivered. "I'd rather you turned into a werewolf."

"Betty Sue or a werewolf? Are you giving me a choice of lobotomy or lycanthropy?"

"I don't want you to be either one. I just want you to be your lovable, kookie self."

"Thank you—I guess," she said doubtfully.

Clifford stood up. "Let's go see about Aunt Charlotte and then go for a nice, long walk."

Aunt Charlotte was just waking up when they went into the living room. Clifford turned on a big Satsuma lamp beside the sofa.

On her craggy old face was the classic bewilderment of a drunk waking up in a strange place. She looked at the sofa and then squinted into the lamp's brightness. Then she looked at Clifford and Dinah.

"The most peculiar thing. I seem to have had an attack of vertigo."

"May I suggest coffee and tomato juice?" said Clifford.

"You've seen attacks of this kind before, Clifford?" she quavered.

"Frequently. I'll tell you flat out, man-to-man, or nephew-to-aunt; you were drunk, Aunt Charlotte."

She sat up and tried to look indignant but only succeeded in looking sodden and forlorn. "How can you say such an idiotic thing? You know I don't drink."

"It was an accident," he told her soothingly. "Your glass was beside Gilly's on the coffee table and you picked up the wrong one."

"But I would have tasted the difference," she argued.

"Vodka doesn't have much taste, and it was mixed with several different kinds of fruit juice."

She regarded him with the trepidation of one whose last waking hours are now an alcoholic blur.

"Clifford, was I—did I?"

"Your behavior was exemplary," he assured her heartily.

"It was a rather euphoric feeling," she mused. "Not altogether unpleasant."

"As many before you have discovered." He leaned over and patted her arm. "Now, how about that coffee?"

"Water first," she creaked. "Ice water. Then coffee."

She smiled faintly. "You're a thoughtful boy, Clifford. Not like your brothers."

"I should hope not. And I appreciate this unsolicited, spontaneous testimonial. Especially in Dinah's presence."

Slowly regaining her faculties, Aunt Charlotte glanced from Dinah to Clifford. Comprehension dawned in her bleary eyes.

He put his arm around Dinah's shoulder. "Dinah has consented to become my bride, in a manner of speaking."

"What on earth do you mean—'in a manner of speaking'?"

"I mean she doesn't like big weddings. Or small weddings. And neither do I."

"Actually, I don't either," said Aunt Charlotte. "Your brothers' weddings gave me a positive revulsion for such affairs."

"Vulgar competitions in money spending," said Clifford.

The phone rang, and Dinah went into the hall to answer it. It was David, bubbling over with the afternoon's developments.

"Dinah, I have you to thank for getting Sterling interested in Midtown real estate."

"I really think it was his idea," she demurred modestly. "At least he was off and running as soon as I mentioned it. And Gilly pitched in and egged him on."

"I thought it was just an idle whim of the rich," he went on excitedly. "Then he called me a while ago, still wanting to buy those wretched houses."

"I don't want to dampen your spirits, but have you seen the inside?"

"No, is it bad?"

"Absolutely the worst. But don't fret yourself, David. The more awful it is, the more of a challenge it will be to him."

"I need you and Gilly to join us. Keep his thoughts running in that vein. I called the woman who owns them, and she's willing to sell. I'm going out now to get the keys from her. Could you meet us there at ten o'clock tomorrow morning?"

"Be happy to. I can't stay long, though. We're taking Aunt Charlotte to see Ted and Amanda's shop."

"Some day one of those junk piles in that place is going to topple and crush somebody," he predicted cheerfully.

While he talked, she heard a clinking sound, like wind chimes.

"David, what are you doing?"

"What am I doing how?"

"That clinking noise you're making."

"Oh," he laughed. "Tapping my pen on the phone. I didn't know I was doing it. It's a sign I'm nervous."

"Well, don't be. I'm sure he's going to buy. And if he doesn't, someone else will."

"That's my Dinah," he said. "Always spreading sunshine."

"What's she like; the woman who owns those houses?" Dinah asked, partly from a mild curiosity and partly to steer him away from expressions like "my Dinah" when she had just been spoken for.

"I haven't met her but she sounds respectable. I don't know much about her except that she owns a jewelry store. Her name is Marie Castle. The important thing is she's willing to sell and wants me as her agent."

"To add to her ill-gotten gains," Dinah commented bitterly. "What sort of person would turn a gang of bikers loose on a neighborhood?"

"Now, now," said David, springing to Mrs. Castle's defense because of that admirable frame of mind—a willingness to sell. "I gather her husband handled the rental property. Then she got those two houses in the divorce settlement and now wants to get rid of them and the bikers."

"Well, whoever rented to them, the results are pretty awesome," said Dinah. "You'll see tomorrow."

She told him good-by and looked up to see Clifford standing beside her.

"David," she said, "wants me and Gilly to meet him at those houses tomorrow to help him in his sales spiel."

"It takes a heap of living to get a house in that shape," he remarked. "Or living in a heap."

He took her hands. "Aunt Charlotte is recovering with coffee and tomato juice. Amanda seems to be still sleeping. Let's go before the next wave of company hits here."

Outside, they stood at the edge of the porch. Mimosa Way looked peaceful, somnolent, houses and trees silverplated with a dreamlike luminosity, partly from the moon but mostly from the fiercely bright street lights installed by the city to deter crime.

They descended the steps in silence.

On the sidewalk, Clifford drew a deep breath. "How nice it is to get out in the fresh carbon monoxide after being cooped up all day in a house full of alcohol fumes."

They held hands and strolled along in contented silence, in the direction they had taken in the morning to look for Aunt Charlotte.

In front of the winos' house, Clifford said, "Want to go through the alley?"

Dinah shivered. "Never again if I can help it."

At the corner, a burst of laughter from Clifford was startling in the Sunday night stillness.

"What on earth . . . ?" she began.

"I just had an alarming thought. What if Aunt Charlotte, after discovering the healing oblivion of alcohol, should become a late-bloomer and take to 'the drink' as she calls it?"

Dinah joined in his laughter. "I can see her twirling around on a bar stool at Custer's Last Stand bellowing to the bartender that the next round is on her."

"Yet such things have happened," said Clifford solemnly. "And what could I tell my brothers? We'd have to hide it from them as long as possible—till they came down to see what was keeping her.

"How I wish Hardin could have seen her this afternoon. He is just about the prissiest son-of-a-bitch you'll ever meet. He is the only person I know who has turned moderation into a vice. He makes a big show of taking one drink —only one, and then putting his hand over his glass and making some putrid joke about having to drive home because Betty Sue's too drunk. And wait," he went on dolefully, "until you meet her. Drunkenness would improve her personality one hundred per cent."

He sighed. "I'm afraid you will have to meet them, Dinah. But I promise I won't inflict them on you longer than it takes for a few hurried amenities. We'll go up for a weekend and give them a glimpse of the bride."

"Clifford, how did you turn out so different from the others?"

"Well, you know my parents died about two years apart when I was twelve and fourteen. Aunt Charlotte took me over, but it wasn't the same somehow. She was getting on in years, and she's never been the disciplinarian she likes to think she is. Actually, I did as I pleased as long as I pretended to follow her rules. And you had pretty much the same thing. How old were you?"

She knew he meant when her parents were killed in a highway accident. "I was nine. And if lack of discipline really bred criminals, I'd be another Bonnie Parker by now."

They walked past the front of the three walled villas whose back gardens they had seen from the alley that morning. Surrounded as they were by derelict neighbors, they gave the appearance of structures built to withstand siege, like castle keeps.

As they reached the entrance of the alley around the corner on Fern Terrace, a figure emerged from a clump of shrubbery behind the garage of the corner house. It was Tim Dobson, the wino who had discovered Artie Stockton's body.

It seemed remarkable for him to be sober until she reflected that while less-dedicated drinkers get drunk to cushion shock, drown sorrow, or celebrate, Tim reacted to emotional upheavals with a spell of sobriety.

He advanced toward them with a finger held dramatically to his lips. Dinah was aware for the first time of his odd reversion to respectability when he was sober. Without his white overalls—which were a sort of drinking uniform—and dressed in sport shirt and slacks, he had a look of offbeat distinction. He was tall and slender. His face had the esthetic look of someone who has dedicated his life to good works—a probation officer or minister of some minor sect. She recalled hearing someone say that he was from a fairly well-to-do family.

When he was close enough to whisper, he pointed to the dark houses. "There's somebody in there."

"How do you know?" Dinah whispered.

"He's got a flashlight. He's not keeping it on; just turning it on for a couple of seconds at a time."

"We must call the police," said Dinah. "But how? He could get away while we're going to phone."

"We can stay here and watch while you go phone," said Clifford.

Dinah glanced across the street at Gilly's apartment. "Gilly's lights are on."

"Go quick then," whispered Clifford. "Don't get trapped in a long conversation."

"I'll go round to the back and you can watch the front," Tim told him.

"Which house is he in?"

"This one—on the alley."

Dinah went across, unhurriedly, in case he might be looking out the window. Gilly's apartment was on the first floor. She rang the bell and kept on ringing. She could hear voices on the radio or TV inside. Where was Gilly?

Remembering that the prowler might be looking out of one of the darkened windows, she had to restrain herself from running back across the street. She saw Clifford standing in front of the garage, out of sight of anyone looking out of the windows of the bikers' house.

"Gilly doesn't answer the bell," she told him in a breathless whisper. "The TV or radio is on. She must be asleep. I think it will be quicker to go around the corner to the telephone booth. Save explanations, even at my house."

Clifford agreed and told her once again to hurry, but not until she was out of sight of the house they were watching.

At the corner, she remembered she hadn't told Clifford who Tim was.

In the phone booth, a bearded young man was talking. She recognized him as one of the students who routed Aunt Charlotte and Clifford with the firecrackers. She'd have to go home, wasting valuable time and probably running into Aunt Charlotte or Amanda.

Then she heard a babble of voices in the next block and

saw a crowd of people gathered in the street around a couple of police cars. They were parked across and up the street, surrounded by a noisy group of people and dogs. A voice from the police car radios blared out into the night. It was a scene which should have been confined within the borders of a TV screen.

Drawing closer, she saw several bloblike figures in the hilltop yard of Flo's house, flowing together like one of those modern sculptures called "Family Group" or some such nonsense.

The crowd was a fair representation of Mimosa Way residents—drunk derelicts, senile pensioners, college professors and students, and a dozen or so young men and women who worked in downtown offices but were now dressed in the neighborhood costumes of faded jeans and granny dresses.

The dogs were possibly even more polytypical—a Saint Bernard and a white poodle on leashes and six or seven dogs of such mixed ancestry for so many generations that no mark of any breed could be seen on them.

"Do your *Swan Lake* number, Flo," shouted one of the more sophisticated spectators whom she recognized as an economics professor who lived next door to Flo.

"Take it off," yelled an over-alled man of far simpler intellect.

She was close enough now to separate the blur of forms into a couple of blue-clad cops and an unclad Flo. The policemen were trying to wrap what appeared to be a king-size blue bedspread around the fluidly resistant masses of Flo.

She looked down at David Winthrop's house two doors down from Flo's. It was small, exquisite and Victorian—dormered, fan-lighted, gingerbreaded, with twin stained glass windows on either side of the front door. It was also dark, except for a burglar light he usually left on in a bathroom. Then she remembered that he said he was going to get the keys to the bikers' houses from the owner.

The economics professor strolled over to her and Dinah gasped, "Ken, I'm looking for a policeman."

She realized the idiocy of this declaration even before he said, "You are practically surrounded by a cordon of them."

Two more cops were emerging from one of the police cars to lend reinforcement to the beleaguered pair on the hill.

The partisanship of the crowd was becoming more blatant. It was clearly a pep rally for Flo.

"Hang in there, Flo," yelled a young man in a Byronic costume of open-collared white silk shirt and dark trousers.

"Right on, Flo, baby!" cried a girl in a granny dress and floppy-brimmed hat of the type called a "picture hat" in the 1930s.

Dinah grabbed a passing policeman's arm and shouted, "Please come with me. We need a policeman."

As he turned to look inquiringly and somewhat suspiciously at her, she went on quickly, "Around the corner. There's someone prowling around with a flashlight in one of the bikers' houses. I left two friends watching the outside."

He conferred with his partner. "Says there's a prowler in one of those houses where the biker was killed."

The other's reply was lost in the uproar. He turned back to Dinah. "Come on. Get in."

She climbed into the back seat and the two policemen got in the front.

The crowd mistook their departure for retreat. "The fuzz is on the run," shouted one of Flo's fans. A cheer went up. Dinah wondered if the cops wrestling with Flo also thought their buddies had deserted them.

Clifford was not alone. As the police car sped down Fern Terrace, she saw two people standing with him in front of the garage.

The policemen pulled up in front of the house and Dinah saw that Clifford's companions were Jane Walker, leader of the Grass Menagerie, and one of her musicians. Jane was wearing an ankle-length paisley cotton dress. Her long, ash-blond hair was gathered at the back in a demure, waist-length pony tail. Dinah thought she looked more like a character from *Little Women* than the leader of a rock group who had spent the night in jail.

Her companion was a short, stocky youth whose small face was completely surrounded by what looked like a Christmas wreath of dark curly hair. Imprinted on the front of his white T-shirt was the puzzling exhortation to "Keep on trucking." His blue jeans were worn and faded and patched to a fashionable state of dilapidation.

"We were thinking of going in, Dinah," Jane whispered. "There's enough of us."

"Not unless one of you has a gun," admonished one of the cops.

"Oh, I don't mean storming the place," she told him scornfully. "Sneaking in was what we had in mind."

"Do you think he's in there?" one of the policemen asked Clifford.

"I saw the flashlight once about five minutes ago. For a few seconds at the back of the house, probably in the kitchen. And it was pretty dim. Either had his hand over it or the batteries are getting low."

"We better split up and one go around to the back," said the driver of the police car.

The other said, "I'll be glad to go. I'd rather tangle with a killer than that fat lady any day."

As one cop disappeared around the corner of the house, the other said, "I'm going to take a look in that alley. He might have gone out the back."

Dinah said, "Clifford, have you heard anything from Tim—the man who's guarding the back?"

"No, but I imagine he understands that a stakeout must be quiet—a rule we out front seem to have forgotten."

"Where," he asked, "did you find the cops? Or is it the better part of valor not to ask?"

"Flo was doing her dance. Two other cops were trying to wrap a bedspread around her, and these two were just about to go to their aid—or rescue—when I snagged them. There was a crowd collected, all rooting for Flo."

"Too many people around here call the cops about things that aren't any of their business," Jane commented darkly. "Flo doesn't bother anybody and it's her own yard."

"I know a well-known sociologist who agrees heartily with you," Dinah told her. "She lives in that yellow apartment over there."

Reminded of Gilly, she said to Clifford, "I wonder where she is. She couldn't have gone far because the radio or TV was on."

She forgot about the problem of Gilly's whereabouts when the cop who had gone to see about Tim reappeared.

"Guy's out cold back there," he told them. "Got to get an ambulance."

He hurried to the police car and pulled a microphone off a dashboard clip to talk into it.

Rejoining them, he asked Dinah, "You know this guy?"

"How can I know until I see him? I know the man who went back there to watch the back exit until the police came."

Nobody said anything further until they reached the man lying on the ground in front of one of the derelict refrigerators. Of course it was Tim.

The policeman said, "This the one who was guarding the back?"

"Yes. Tim Dobson. He's also the one who found Artie Stockton's body this morning. But there's nothing suspicious about it; he lives at the other end of the alley."

"I didn't say there was anything suspicious," he told her in an elaborately mild tone which implied that all of it was very suspicious indeed.

They looked down to see Tim struggling to a sitting position. He said weakly, "He came at me like a whirlwind. Hit me with something. Must have been the flashlight."

"What did he look like?" asked the policeman.

Tim looked dazedly around at the sea of junk and then at the policeman. "He looked like a biker, but I'm damn sure he wasn't. Had on a black stocking mask. Scary-looking. And one of those black fringed jackets and those black caps they wear. But his shirt and pants weren't black. Looked more like gray or green."

The policeman said, "No hope you could tell anything about his face with a stocking mask. But what about his body?"

Tim clasped his hands around his knees as if he were cozily chatting with one of his cronies. "He looked like he was in good shape. Young. Or not old, anyway. And he was about my height—around six feet."

The cop said, "What happened to Chance?"

"Chance?" Dinah echoed bewilderedly, since he seemed to be addressing her.

"My partner."

"He went that way," she pointed down the alley.

"I went down that alley soon as I found this guy and I didn't see him." His tone was faintly accusatory.

Dinah said, "I assure you I'm not hiding him. Maybe he's gone down the other alley; the one behind here."

"I better go find him," he muttered, apparently to himself, and took off down the alley.

Tim tried to stand up and Dinah shoved him back down with her hands on his shoulders. "You'd better not move around until they find out about that blow on your head."

Sirens approached. Dinah cautioned Tim again not to move, went back around to the front, and saw the ambulance and Mark Latham arriving at the same time.

Chapter Thirteen

Mark heard the details from Dinah and Clifford as they strode around to the back. The ambulance attendants followed with a stretcher.

The two patrol car policemen came back to report that they had found each other but no one else.

And then, of course, a crowd gathered, drawn by the lure of sirens from the white ambulance with its revolving red light on top, making, thought Dinah, a patriotic display behind the two white police cars with winking blue lights.

Some she recognized as people who had been watching Flo, and others erupted from nearby houses and apartments, banging doors and talking excitedly.

It occurred to Dinah that these gatherings were rather like block parties in more conventional neighborhoods. People lingered on a few minutes after the official vehicles had departed to exchange news and gossip.

Mark walked behind the men carrying the stretcher on which Tim lolled like a Roman emperor, head propped on one hand and waving to the crowd with the other.

Mark stopped beside Dinah and Clifford. "I can't figure out what he wanted in this dump. We searched it good and took out all the weapons and drugs."

"What kind of drugs?" asked Dinah.

"Mostly pot. We didn't find any heroin, but didn't really expect to. It's far too valuable to leave lying around loose in a place like this. I doubt if the big boss lets them have much of it at a time."

"Who is that?" she asked.

"We don't know," he admitted unhappily. "It's a new one. One was arrested about six months ago, and is now in the Federal pen. But there are always others.

"Stick around a few minutes, will you? I want to see how he got in."

The two uniformed cops went around to the back, and Mark walked up on the front porch, turned the knob and opened the door.

The rest of the crowd stood a little apart from them, suspicious of anybody seen talking to the cops, on the grounds that they must be either cops themselves or robbers.

Mark came back. "He went in the front door and left it unlocked. Wasn't planning on being disturbed. We locked up when we left here this morning. So he has a key."

"That narrows it down somewhat then," said Clifford.

Mark smiled. "In your house or mine it would. But there were about forty of 'em living here, plus visitors from other places. We got one from the Detroit chapter when we hauled 'em in."

"On what charge?" asked Clifford.

"Possession of drugs, stolen goods, stolen guns. Material witnesses to murder."

Dinah looked up to see Gilly, in slacks and old shirt, hurrying across the street.

When she reached the curb, Dinah said, "Where have you been? I rang your bell about twenty minutes ago."

"I was asleep. What's going on here?"

Dinah and Clifford told her.

"I can't imagine how I missed it," she complained. "I was sitting in front of the television and dozed off. Must have thought all the racket was a TV show."

Some of the other onlookers, tiring of the inaction, began drifting off, leaving a dozen or so divided into three groups.

A new Chrysler Imperial pulled up behind the police cars. David Winthrop was at the wheel and a woman sat beside him. Since David's car was a two-year-old Buick, the car must belong to the woman.

He got out to go around and open the other door and asked the popular question, "What's going on here?"

Weary of the long narrative, Dinah shortened it to, "Somebody was prowling around in one of these houses."

The woman got out. A shadowy figure inside the car, she blossomed under the street light into a stunning blonde, casually but expensively dressed in slacks and silk shirt which showed off her salient features. All good, Dinah noted, and so did the men.

Dinah also noted that something about her suggested she wasn't quite "quality," as Amanda's generation so quaintly put it. For one thing, she was wearing a quantity of jewelry befitting an early Egyptian princess—several necklaces and strands of beads, clusters of rings, and a couple of bracelets from which dangled a jangling collection of charms and coins. Allowing for the fact that owning a jewelry store would present a lot of temptation to bedizenment, there should be some sort of limit for yielding to it.

David introduced her as Marie Castle, owner of the two houses.

He said to Mark, "Mrs. Castle wants to sell those houses. I'm planning to show them tomorrow. We figured we'd better come over and see what shape they're in."

"Bad," Mark told him bluntly. "Very bad indeed. Take my word for it. In fact, you'll have to—take my word for it, I mean. Somebody was looking for something in there and we want to search it again."

"But I have an appointment to show it to a good prospect at ten in the morning," David protested.

"We'll be through before then," said Mark. And to Mrs. Castle, "Do you have any idea how many keys there are to these houses?"

She pondered prettily, in the fashion model's manner, without disarranging her face. "I have no idea. My husband—ex-husband, that is—handled rental property. I know he gave out only one key to each house, but they could have had a lot of them made from that."

"Aside from the tenants, most or all of which are in jail, do you know of any other keys besides your own?"

"My husband could have kept a set and given me duplicates. I don't know."

"You and your husband had other property?"

"Yes, two apartments and our house. We worked out the financial settlement ourselves. The two apartments to him, and these houses and our house to me. I've done rather well in my business and I had already paid for these and part of our house."

"Yes, your jewelry shop," said Mark. "My wife has bought several things there that she likes very much."

She bestowed a smile on him. Then the implication of the knowledge behind the compliment hit her. "How did you know?"

"We usually find out who the owners are of houses that

require a lot of our attention," he said easily. "May I ask where the two apartments are—the ones your husband got in the settlement?"

Looking puzzled and uneasy, she told him the addresses in Inman Park and Morningside.

Defensively, she said, "They're not rented to bikers. My husband didn't know what these people were before they moved in. They sent a couple of girls to rent the houses. They looked all right. And in Atlanta you can't evict tenants for any reason except not paying the rent."

Gilly, who had been a hostile listener, said, "Also, you can give them notice to move because you're going to remodel or improve the place. But when you're getting four hundred or five hundred dollars apiece for houses like this, who needs improvement?"

Dinah, standing with her back to the cluster of neighbors, felt a prickling along the back of her neck, as if some atavistic sense had detected the stirring of a slumbering beast. The neighbors had stopped talking and had drawn closer to listen.

Mark caught on, too. He drifted, or tried to give the appearance of drifting, over to talk to them.

Gilly said, "Why don't we go over to my place for a drink or a cup of tea or something?"

It was an odd assortment, Dinah thought, trooping over to Gilly's. Feeling some sort of vague obligation to Mark, she lagged behind to invite him over to join them.

"Thanks, Dinah. I'll come over in a few minutes." As she continued to linger, he added by way of dismissal, "Tell Gilly I'll be over."

But an old lady named Mrs. Robbins drew her into the conversation. "Do you know that woman?" she asked Dinah.

"Mrs. Castle? No, I've never seen her before."

"Well, we have. Don't let her tell you any lies about how her husband managed these houses and she didn't know anything about it. We've seen her over here talking to those bikers."

Mark seemed to be assuming the skeptic's role to egg her on. "Maybe she came over to collect the rent when her husband was sick or out of town."

As he had no doubt expected, this naïve view was met with the scorn it richly deserved.

"Mr. Summers knows. Tell them, Ansell," Mrs. Robbins instructed a bald, bespectacled man.

"I've seen her go in there three times over the last year and stay a good while—thirty or forty minutes. Once was at eleven o'clock at night.

"She answered the phone several times when Lavinia or I called to ask them to get rid of those—" he seemed handicapped either by extreme emotion or the presence of women. "She was real smart-ass about it. Told me one time if I didn't like it, why didn't I move?"

His voice trembled with rage. "I told her I'd like to see her try to sell my house with that gang of bikers living two doors away. I watch 'em all the time I can. And I've made some inquiries about that fancy-looking Mrs. Castle. Why don't you ask her about all those trips to Mexico?"

Mark, carrying obtuseness almost to the point of imbecility, said blandly, "She owns a jewelry store, you know. My wife has bought some things from her. Some of it Mexican stuff—silver and turquoise and jade. Mrs. Castle told her she goes down there every two or three months."

"And meets somebody," declared Mr. Summers. "She goes to Laredo or one of those places where you can just walk across the border, and buys jewelry and picks up something else to smuggle across."

"Mr.—ah—Summers, isn't it?—how do you know all this?"

"I have ways of finding out, and if I could find out, seems like the cops could, too—if they wanted to," he added slanderously.

Mark ignored the slur. "We'll certainly look into it. I appreciate your telling me this. We need more public-spirited citizens like you to come forward with information."

This remark, as it was intended to do, produced a spirited rivalry in displays of good citizenship.

"There's somebody else comes here in the middle of the night," announced a desiccated ancient in a hybrid costume of trousers, pajama top, and leather bedroom slippers.

Mark wisely remained silent but interested.

"He comes in a taxi or on foot," his informant continued in a quavering voice. "I've seen him maybe five or six times. He wears a beard and dark glasses and a hat and big raincoat."

"What does he do?" asked Mark.

"Do? Why he goes up and knocks on the door and somebody lets him in."

"When did you last see him here?"

"A week ago. Ten days, maybe."

"Was he in a taxi that time?"

"Yes, sir. A yellow cab."

"What time of night?"

"It was around midnight, but sometimes it's later—one or two."

"I've seen him, too, and I live closer than he does,"

declared Mrs. Robbins, making her entry into the good citizenship contest. "I live next door. And also," she added as a clincher, "my eyesight is better than his."

"Who says so?" demanded the senior citizen. "I ain't got bifocals yet, like some who have 'em and won't wear 'em half the time."

"About what age is he?" asked Mark, heading off a presbyopic tournament.

"Well, he sure ain't got rheumatism," said the old man enviously. "He moves quick, like somebody not more'n forty."

Mark asked if anyone else had seen him, hoping, thought Dinah, to get the viewpoint of someone young enough not to regard forty as the beginning of boyhood.

A mannish-looking young woman spoke up—reluctantly, Dinah felt. "I had him for a fare once, about four or five months ago. I drive a yellow cab. I don't generally drive at night, but some of the night drivers were off sick that night.

"It was about midnight," she went on. "I was about to go off duty, and I didn't want to take him, but he said he wasn't going far."

"Where did you pick him up?"

"On Peachtree, in front of the Fox Theater."

"He really wasn't going far," Mark commented. "You must have got a pretty good look at him."

"Well, no matter how close you got to him, you couldn't tell much about his looks in that get-up."

"What about his voice? And his hands?"

"He talked in a hoarse voice, like he had a sore throat or something. He gave me the creeps. Those dark glasses and the hat and beard. I felt like it was a disguise and he might be planning to rob me.

"I didn't notice his hands when he paid the fare. I was so glad to get rid of him. He tipped me fifty cents and I drove off fast. Funny, too. It's right across from my apartment, and I remember thinking I was sure glad he didn't know I lived there."

"Which house did he go in?"

"He was starting toward that one, the one on the alley, but I didn't hang around long enough to see him go in."

Mark encouraged her to enlarge on the feeling of creepiness. But she was not a fanciful woman. It was just plain common sense that anybody wearing all that stuff to hide his face, head, and body was up to no good. She was just glad that whatever it was didn't include robbing and mugging taxi drivers.

No one else responded to Mark's adroit prodding. If anybody else had seen this blatantly suspicious character, nobody was going to admit it.

As the neighbors began to drift homeward, Dinah decided that if the taxi driver hadn't spoken up, she would have suspected that the other two had made him up.

His disguise seemed designed to call attention to himself. Yet it had accomplished its purpose, for no one could describe anything about him except the vaudevillian components of his disguise.

Why hadn't he simply gone to the house as himself? It would have attracted far less attention. And if he was afraid of being recognized, why didn't he arrange to meet Artie Stockton somewhere else? He could have instructed the biker to wear ordinary clothes and no one would have noticed either of them. Particularly if he didn't want the other bikers to know who he was.

"Mark," she whispered, "ask them which way he went when he left the house?"

Mark asked Mrs. Robbins and the old man, and got a surprising answer. No one had seen him leave the bikers' house.

"One of the bikers, you suppose?" Dinah asked as she and Mark started across the street.

To her intense annoyance, he let her know he wasn't going to exchange speculations with her by declaring, "Curiouser and curiouser."

"Or," she persisted, "did he go in the front door in that silly disguise and out the back door as himself?"

Mark smiled indulgently at her, increasing her irritation. "I wish I knew."

"Or maybe," she said, ignoring this evasion, "he didn't want Artie Stockton to know who he was. That must be it.

"But," she went on excitedly, "Artie found out who he was and started blackmailing him."

Since Mark continued his maddening unresponsiveness, she was really thinking aloud. "Why would he be forced to go to the house? If Mrs. Castle buys the stuff in Mexico along with her silver bangles—" She broke off this soliloquy on the steps of Gilly's apartment, on the grounds that Mrs. Castle was inside and it would be bad manners to keep on speaking of her as a criminal.

Gilly greeted them with forthright curiosity. "Where have you been?"

"Talking to some of the bystanders," said Mark.

Gilly's apartment was a shining example of the scholar's unawareness of such trivia as interior decorating. The apartment was not bare. It contained a great many things, mostly of a starkly utilitarian nature. Two studio couches against opposite walls were covered with Indian cotton spreads. Against another wall stood a roll-top desk, its top rolled up to reveal a conglomeration of papers and notebooks massed like flood-washed trash around an old office typewriter. The walls' only adornment were black-framed maps displaying the old-fashioned cartography and type faces of maps cut from old *National Geographics.*

Completing the room's decor were chairs, tables, and lamps bought at the Good Will or found on trash piles and representing periods from late Victorian to early depression.

The room was pleasantly scented with the oriental fragrance of jasmine tea in a fine old Mason's ironstone tea set with numerous cracks and chips which Gilly had bought from Ted and Amanda. And, of course, she was extolling the analeptic powers of jasmine tea.

"Also," she added in a burst of dolorous frankness, "I'm out of gin and whiskey. Not a drop of alcohol in the place."

Mark discarded his policeman's mien and became his social self, genial and restrainedly jovial. After the spate of incriminating revelations out in the street, Dinah thought he was being acutely observant under his relaxed air. It was Marie Castle in whom he was interested, and therefore in whom he showed the least interest. As she was a lady accustomed to intense interest from men, Dinah thought he might be overdoing it just a little.

Mrs. Castle sat between David and Clifford on one of the studio couches. Mark sat in a Victorian rocker, replete with knobs, spindles, and carved protrusions, placed in a strategic spot between the two sofas.

Dinah, on the other studio couch with Jane and her companion, thought it one of the oddest groups she'd seen lately. But no group was odd to Gilly.

"Jane and I have been discussing the problem of Flo," she informed Dinah and Mark. "The way we see it, however, the problem is not her little pastime of nude dancing but the fact that one or more small-minded neighbors feel impelled to call the police."

"Oh, yes, one of the patrolmen was telling me about it," said Mark. "I agree with you from a police viewpoint. Tonight it tied up two patrolmen who were needed elsewhere."

"Like here," said Jane. "But I can't figure out who could have called the police. It was always an old lady who lived a couple of doors away, and she moved about a month ago."

David said, "It is puzzling, come to think of it. Everybody else in our block is blessed with an almost Babylonian tolerance. I can't think of anybody else who'd call them."

"Maybe somebody passing by," Mark suggested. "She sounds like a traffic stopper."

"Maybe so," said David. "Or somebody new we don't know yet."

Dinah's attention focused on Marie Castle, daintily sipping tea, the movements of her slender arms accompanied by the jangle of bracelets. Clifford was also focusing attention on her, but not with the concentration he had devoted to Betty last night.

Was it only last night? It seemed like several months ago.

Could Marie Castle actually be in league with a gang of bikers? Or was she a victim of slander from an embittered neighborhood?

Not necessarily intentional slander, she thought. The people on this block of Fern Terrace, led by Mrs. Robbins and Mr. Summers, were understandably angry about having a gang of bikers for neighbors. And the distilled essence of their hatred was concentrated on the owners who had rented to them. She was sure they sincerely believed the things they'd told Mark. After a few shocked protests, you can believe scandalous things about the people you like. The people you don't like are capable of anything.

The silver-blond woman was a type not too familiar to Dinah. The few people she knew who had risen from one class to another were slaves to propriety—in dress, behavior, and such possessions as houses and cars.

Mrs. Castle, with her too-stylish clothes and her too-correct manners, appeared jarringly out of place in Gilly's apartment. Someone as securely fixed in her orbit as Gilly can flout rules and mores. The upwardly mobile, as Gilly's profession labeled them, cannot.

She tuned back in on the conversation. David was asking again if the two houses would be open by ten tomorrow morning. He looked preoccupied and worried. Martin Sterling's interest in the neighborhood could mean a lot of sales for him.

He at least seemed impervious to Marie Castle's sensational looks. Dinah reflected cynically that if Freud had had his head together and had ventured out of his study more often, he'd have caught on that sex nearly always runs a poor second to money.

"Never you fear," Mark assured him.

"You're planning to search it tonight then?"

Mark stood up. "Right away, in fact. Thanks for the tea, Gilly."

She went with him to the door, sending her regards to Beverly and Ivy.

David said, "I wonder if maybe we should postpone showing him the houses until we can get them cleaned up. Those mattresses and clothes and the writing on the wall—" He seemed to be addressing this anxious query to the room at large, but Gilly answered.

"No. Clean them up, and what will they be? Just a couple of dreary depression houses with no more architectural appeal than a McDonald's. The horror of it is their only charm. Think of the wonderful 'before' and 'after' pictures he'll have to show to his friends and loved ones."

David's face brightened. "That's a great idea. Will you suggest it, Gilly?"

"Be glad to."

As the other four got up to leave, Dinah remembered Amanda's theory which she called Prentiss' law of multiple departure: that one person getting up to go home will start a mass exodus. In the stampede you think everybody's left until you look around and see one or two people—usually a notorious bore and/or an obnoxious drunk who have settled in to stay till dawn.

When the others had left, Gilly said, "At last. We can eat. I have just enough roast left for three sandwiches."

Chapter Fourteen

They followed Gilly to the kitchen, another room with unusual furnishings. A glass-doored bookcase was full of oddments collected in Gilly's travels. On top of the bookcase stood a large and gaudily besequined plaster bluebird which Gilly had won in a shooting gallery at the fair.

On an old wicker rocker, Simon, Gilly's cat, was curled up asleep. He was a cat of many colors and patterns—orange and gray tufts intermixed with black and white stripes. She had found him on the street when he was about six months old, starving and so thin he looked like a cat painted on a sheet of paper.

Dinah said, "Your neighbors were giving Mark an earful. They told him that Marie Castle, far from being an absentee landlady, is actually pretty chummy with the Desperadoes. They think she meets a connection in Mexico to buy drugs—when she goes there to buy jewelry—and brings it back for the bikers to sell."

"I've heard that theory from Mrs. Robbins and Mr. Summers, and I think it's possible," said Gilly, opening the refrigerator and getting out a slender portion of what had once been a large rolled roast.

"Mrs. Castle is a type that interests me," she said.

"There is an Eliza Doolittle quality about her speech and manners."

"I get the same feeling," said Dinah. "That she's worked very hard to improve herself."

"Nothing wrong with that in itself," Gilly declared. "I think the reason people are censorious of social climbers is that most of them try to hide their background and upgrade it. Those who frankly admit it are generally admired."

"Also," said Dinah, "there's a mystery man who comes there in the middle of the night—in dark glasses, a hat and raincoat, and what is probably a false beard."

Reaching in the old cupboard for more chipped cups, Dinah said, "Have you ever seen him, Gilly?"

"No, I'm usually working or reading at night. I haven't been able to join the neighbor-watching society."

"I don't think you'd exactly call it snooping," said Clifford. "How could you help watching neighbors like that?"

Gilly laughed. "Maybe I should have been studying them at night and working in the daytime. I wonder who this mystery man can be."

"I know who Mark thinks he is," said Dinah. "The drug ring boss."

"It makes me feel uneasy," said Gilly. "I think I'm getting to be like those doddering old scholars who mooch about reading Proust and bird watching and never noticing what people are doing."

She struck a thoughtful pose with a big dill pickle held aloft in her hand. "But one can get too bogged down in research. Like that man—what's his name?—who started out to write a gigantic book about sex in America and is still going around to massage parlors and brothels. Too much preoccupation with research can keep you from ever getting started writing."

Dinah took the pickle out of her hand and picked up a knife to slice it. Clifford measured instant coffee into the cups. Gilly came out of her reverie and finished making the sandwiches.

In the living room Gilly said, "What do you think of our neighborhood, Clifford?"

"It's overwhelming."

"I don't know whether that was meant as a compliment or not. I rather think not. But you must admit it's not dull."

"Far from it," he agreed heartily.

"How is your Aunt Charlotte?"

"Hung over," said Dinah. "That was naughty of you, Gilly."

"Does she know I switched the glasses?"

"No, Clifford told her she had picked up your glass by mistake."

"But I think she rather liked it," Clifford said musingly. "Being drunk, I mean. Just think, if Aunt Charlotte were a latent dipsomaniac, your prank might make her into an active one."

"It could be," said Gilly. "I have no patience with the idiots who say that people don't change. People change all the time, sometimes suddenly and drastically."

"I don't know what we'd do with her in Andrewsville," said Clifford. "A drunk Aunt Charlotte staggering down a receiving line at the country club, falling off the podium while she's giving a talk on hardy perennials to the garden club—" He shuddered. "I'm glad I'm not going back."

"Not going back?" said Gilly.

"No, I'm settling down here with Dinah."

Gilly looked astonished. "You mean here—in this neighborhood?"

"Of course. You don't know how to appreciate this lively little community, Gilly. You've never lived in Andrewsville. It's like being smothered to death with finger sandwiches."

"I may never have lived there, but I've spoken to women's clubs in several dozen Andrewsvilles. God forbid that I should ever get stuck in one of them, even for a couple of days."

Dinah laughed. "You wouldn't be stuck long. They'd tar and feather you and haul you to the city limits. You couldn't live anywhere but here, Gilly."

"And I'm glad you're joining us, Clifford," said Gilly. "I sort of suspected that you and Dinah were fixing your attentions on each other, as they used to say at Miss Potter's School for Girls."

"The only thing that surprises me is your decision to stay here. I thought you'd try to persuade Dinah to go back with you. I was a little worried. This girl is a talented writer, and I'm afraid those finger sandwiches would smother her, too."

"They won't get the opportunity," Clifford said firmly.

"Will you buy a house?"

"Probably not right away. Unless Dinah knows of one she likes."

Gilly grinned. "I understand there are two for sale right across the street."

"Save your sales talk for Martin Sterling," said Dinah.

"You told your aunt?" asked Gilly.

"Yes, and her reaction was untypical," Clifford told her. "Turns out she's always hated big weddings, too. Come to think of it, Aunt Charlotte hasn't been acting like herself lately. I mean besides being drunk this afternoon."

"How do you mean?" asked Gilly.

"Well, actually it started about six months ago when she took up with a faith healer."

Gilly displayed the universal reaction to this news by gasping, "Faith healer!"

"Yes," said Clifford. "I felt it was strange, too, until I thought it over and decided that after years of pain for which my doctor offered only aspirin, I'd probably be willing to try anything, too.

"Anyway, this guy has got Aunt Charlotte on a goodwill trip: banish hatred and injustice from your life and you rid your body of the poisons causing pain."

"And Clifford thinks she came down here to turn over Amanda's share of the bobbin rights. She gets part of the income from the bobbin, but Aunt Charlotte's husband left the rights to her."

"I know," said Gilly. "Wonder why she hasn't said anything yet."

"Well, a lot has been going on," Clifford reminded her. "And thanks to you, she was drunk today."

"Oh, dear, I'm sorry. Amanda has been obsessed with those bobbin rights for years. I hope I didn't throw a spanner in the works."

"I'm sure you didn't," said Clifford. "I imagine she's waiting for a good audience without a lot of distractions going on. Aunt Charlotte is not one to slop over with sentiment, but when she does, she wants to get maximum effect."

"Well!" said Gilly. "And what else do you mean, Clifford, about her acting strangely?"

"Well, she hasn't commented on this neighborhood or

any of the things going on here. By that, I mean the normal things somebody like Aunt Charlotte would say about a place like this. She hasn't been her old assertive self."

"I've noticed it, too," Dinah said. "She's been downright charming in a gruff sort of way. Kind of like Smokey the Bear."

Gilly sighed. "The more I see of people, the more I realize I don't know a damn thing about them."

Clifford stood up. "You mustn't admit it outside of these four walls, though."

She laughed. "Ordinarily, I wouldn't admit it inside these four walls."

To Dinah, he said, "We must get back to the matriarchs."

"Oh, yes, Amanda will wake up and wonder where we are."

But Amanda was not awake when they reached the house. A gentle, steady snoring issued from her room as Dinah opened her door an inch or so, and then closed it. Aunt Charlotte's room was also dark.

In the back hall, Dinah and Clifford exchanged brief endearments, then parted to go separately and chastely to bed.

Chapter Fifteen

Dinah was awakened by the domestic sounds of clanging pans and running water in the kitchen.

Just in time to stop the surge of adrenalin necessary for getting up on Monday, she remembered that Miles had given her the day off. Dear Miles, she thought fondly. Sarcastic at times, sometimes given to ranting or sulking over trifles, he was nonetheless one of the better examples of the male sex. He was not only witty himself, he laughed uproariously at the jokes of others.

"What on earth are you smiling about at this hour?" Amanda asked from the kitchen doorway.

"I was thinking of Miles—what a thoroughly nice person he is. How sensitive he is to the needs and feelings of others."

Amanda regarded her wonderingly. "That's not what you were saying about him last week."

"That was last week. This week he has given me Monday off."

"What possessed him to do a thing like that?"

"Our party yesterday," Dinah told her. "Miles loves embarrassing situations—purely as a spectator. And the place was teeming with them. He was in a froth of good will by the time Aunt Charlotte passed out on the sofa. He'd have given me the whole week off if I'd asked."

Amanda seized on the one gloomy aspect of this speech. "Charlotte! Did you see her last night after she woke up and went to her room?"

"I saw her after she woke up and before she went to her room. She didn't remember anything; thought she'd had an attack of vertigo."

Amanda giggled. "I'm sorry I missed it. I got up about ten to get something to eat, but her room was dark so I didn't disturb her."

"Clifford set her straight, though. He told her she was drunk. But he also told her she had picked up the wrong glass by mistake."

"He didn't tell her about Gilly?"

"No. Clifford seems to be exquisitely tactful. Almost as fine a fellow as Miles.

"As a matter of fact," she continued, standing up and wondering how to break the news to Amanda, "I'm getting pretty fond of him."

"Miles?" Amanda's jaw dropped in astonishment. "I hope you haven't forgotten that he's married."

Dinah reached for her robe. "I wonder if you're being deliberately dense. You know I don't mean Miles."

"Then you must mean Clifford." Amanda backed into the kitchen and Dinah followed.

"By a brilliant process of elimination, you've finally got it."

"But you don't mean—do you? Why, you hardly know him."

She considered briefly how to let Amanda know how well she knew Clifford without going into too much detail.

"He's what I've always wanted, Granny. You've never

heard me make that statement about another man, have you?"

"Well, I've heard you make somewhat similar statements. Not quite so positive, though. And I must say he's a very attractive young man. Not at all what I expected."

Dinah said, "Then you'll be happy to have him for a grandson-in-law."

"Grandson!" She shook her head dazedly. "I went to bed too early last night. I missed your entire courtship."

"Think of the bobbin," Dinah said craftily.

Amanda stood in front of the stove, transfixed, as one in a vision, her face lighted with an almost religious fervor.

Dinah laughed. "I can see you are thinking of the bobbin. And I'm ashamed of you, Granny. Most grandmothers would be dreaming of a big wedding and a gigantic reception."

"But, Dinah, you know when I think of the bobbin, I'm thinking of you—your future."

"Your water's boiling," Dinah said prosaically.

Amanda picked up the steaming kettle and poured water in her cup. "Naturally, I can't help thinking that if you had to fall in love in this headlong fashion, you made a fortunate choice. Now it won't matter who Charlotte leaves the bobbin rights to. You'll get your share." She sighed happily, "Aren't you having breakfast?"

"I'm going to wait for Clifford."

Amanda, still stunned, said, "I can't get over it. All this romance seething around me, and I didn't notice a thing. Where did you go last night?"

"To the bikers' houses, and then over to Gilly's."

Amanda said angrily, "This whole thing is too much for me. You're going to sit down and tell me everything that happened after I foolishly went to sleep yesterday afternoon."

While Dinah was telling her, with judicious omissions, Clifford came in, dressed in the gray slacks and navy shirt that had sent her senses reeling Saturday afternoon.

"Good morning," he said cheerily. "Another beautiful day. Perfect weather for murder, breaking and entering, drug pushing—all the neighborhood crafts and hobbies."

"Don't try to change the subject," Dinah said crossly.

"Maybe I could keep to the subject a little better if I knew what it was," he pointed out sensibly.

"Marriage," said Amanda. "Yours and Dinah's, to be precise."

"I'm spreading the word around so you can't back out of it," Dinah told him.

"How can I?" he asked bleakly. "We told Aunt Charlotte. And compared to Aunt Charlotte, Paul Revere was shy and uncommunicative. If she hasn't been on the phone to Andrewsville yet, it's because she had a hangover yesterday."

"What I can't understand," said Amanda, "is how you managed to work in these marriage plans while chasing a prowler in the bikers' houses."

"Around here it seems you must sort of work your personal affairs into the neighborhood activities," said Clifford.

Footsteps warned of Aunt Charlotte's approach, so that when she opened the door, the three of them were staring at her.

"Good morning," she said, somewhat self-consciously. And then to Amanda, "You've heard the news?"

"I've heard so much news that it's used up my attention

span for several days," Amanda declared waspishly. "But I suppose you mean about the children."

"Children," Dinah repeated indignantly. "She means us, Clifford."

"Yes, and I'm very happy about it," said Aunt Charlotte. "But what was the other news?"

They told her while Dinah brought her scrambled eggs, cantaloupe, and coffee, and sat down with her own plate.

Dinah outlined her theory: that the purpose of the disguise was to keep Arthur Stockton and the other bikers from finding out who he was. That he must have left by the back door, taking off his disguise, all of which could be stuffed into his raincoat pockets.

Amanda said, "But if he had Mrs. Castle or somebody as a go-between, why would he need to run the risk of going there?"

"Something prevented her from going there, maybe," said Clifford.

"Her divorce?" suggested Aunt Charlotte, getting into the detective game. "What if she were having to be very circumspect to keep her husband from finding out?"

"A sound idea," Clifford approved.

"What made me mad," said Dinah, "was that I helped Mark a lot by suggesting that he ask the neighbors which way the man went when he left the bikers' house. They said they hadn't seen him leaving. Then Mark turned official on me and wouldn't discuss it at all."

Amanda pushed back her chair and got up. "Fascinating as all this is, I must leave to go earn my bread and butter."

"But you never eat bread and butter, Granny," Dinah reminded her. "It's fattening."

"A trite figure of speech."

And no doubt, thought Dinah, designed to remind Charlotte that while she lived in luxury on the family money, Amanda was forced to grub away at earning a living running a junk shop.

"How fortunate you are in having work to do," said Aunt Charlotte wistfully.

Amanda's exit line was, "Still, it would be nice to have a choice."

Dinah said, "I think I know what's the matter with her, Clifford. I didn't tell her I wasn't going to move to Andrewsville."

"Not move to Andrewsville!" Aunt Charlotte exclaimed as Dinah jumped up to try to catch Amanda before she left the house.

Amanda was opening the front door as Dinah called, "Granny, wait up."

She hurried down the hall. "Did you think Clifford and I were planning to live in Andrewsville?"

"Certainly. The Andrews have always lived in Andrewsville."

"Not these. Clifford says he's good and sick of the place, and wants to live here."

"Here?" Her voice rose to a squeak. "He must be insane."

"That doesn't speak too well for those of us who already live here."

Amanda made an impatient, sweeping gesture. "You know perfectly well what I mean. You've never lived in a place like Andrewsville. There and here are like two different planets."

"But that's what Clifford likes about it. He's always hated Andrewsville."

Amanda shook her head, then smiled. "He must be like

your grandfather. He was different from the rest of them, too."

She put out her hand, and Dinah took it. "I must go. Ted's waiting. You're bringing Charlotte over later?"

"Yes, about eleven-thirty."

She decided to get her clothes out of the closet and dress while Clifford was detained in the kitchen with the prickly chore of explaining to Aunt Charlotte why he was leaving Andrewsville.

When she emerged from the bathroom dressed and ready to go, Clifford was waiting for her in the hall.

He grasped her wrist. "When the going gets rough, cowards get going, don't they?"

"Not at all," she told him haughtily. "If you mean leaving you to explain to Aunt Charlotte. Handling Amanda is my business and Aunt Charlotte is yours."

She looked around. "Where is she?"

"Gone for her walk."

"Oh, no," she gasped. "Clifford, you mustn't let her run around loose by herself. Surely you've caught on by now that Aunt Charlotte is the Little Red Riding Hood of the Polident set."

"It's time she learned to cope with the seamier aspects of life," he declared sternly.

"How did she bear up?"

"Remarkably well. I told you she hasn't been acting like herself. She actually said she could understand why I want to get away from Andrewsville."

"I'm beginning to think there are hidden depths to Aunt Charlotte. Or maybe kinks is a better word. But we'll have to talk about that later," she said. "I promised David I'd meet him at the bikers'."

In front of the bikers' houses, a foursome milled about

on the sidewalk. David and Marie Castle and Martin Sterling and an elegantly dressed young man with a handlebar mustache. They were talking in a desultory fashion and glancing every few seconds at the two houses.

Clifford said in a low voice, "They seem to be waiting for something."

"I'm sure it's not us," she whispered.

"Something else in there, maybe? A giant Vampire bat?"

"What a baroque imagination you have, Clifford."

"You don't have to imagine baroque things around here. It's all real."

David seemed glad to see them. Dinah thought he might be badly in need of reinforcements.

The young man splendidly attired in dove-gray slacks, a checkered gray sport coat, and gray shirt with flowered stripes was Ralph Swinton, the architect for Sterling Enterprises.

"Why are you hanging around out here?" asked Dinah.

"Mr. Margolius is in there," David said with a forced jauntiness which failed to hide his anxiety.

Dinah looked at Martin Sterling and immediately detected the absence of yesterday's insouciance. He was staring fixedly at the wreckage of broken concrete, jagged window panes, piled-up refuse, and enveloping deposits of dirt that had settled over both houses like ash from a maniacally active volcano.

He looked, thought Dinah, more dismayed than enraptured. It was time for one of Gilly's little pep talks.

The thought had scarcely taken shape in her mind when Gilly emerged, genielike, from the yellow-brick apartment. Clad in gray wool slacks, white shirt, and blue sweater, all of which had seen much good wear, she managed to look scholarly and distinguished, yet indigenous, like an elderly Salvation Army lass on duty in a home for derelicts.

Her bracing "Good morning" was for the assemblage, but her target was Sterling. She stopped beside him and smilingly said, "Awful, isn't it?" in the same tone of most people exclaiming, "Beautiful, isn't it?"

He brightened. "Yes. Yes, indeed it is."

"Shall we go inside, David?" said Gilly.

David rallied slightly and said, "Yes, in a minute. The housing inspector is in there now. About to finish up, I think."

"Ah, yes, the good Mr. Margolius," she said. "He has confessed with refreshing candor that he's always been afraid to go in there while Our Gang was in residence."

In defensive tones, Marie Castle said, "Well, that was part of our trouble. We didn't know what they were when my husband rented to them. And once they moved in we couldn't get them out, could we, David?"

David said, "That's true. I think the law is very unfavorable to landlords. The only grounds for evicting tenants is non-payment of rent. It doesn't matter what else they're doing."

"Especially if they're paying ridiculously high rent to offset their undesirability as tenants," said Gilly.

Marie was good and mad and trying to keep calm—and also genteel, thought Dinah. For gentility, to those who have acquired it latterly and laboriously, must be always precarious.

The front door of the house on the alley opened, and they all stared at it with the intensity of first-nighters at the opening curtain.

Mr. Margolius emerged. A tall, slender man of about

fifty with an air of melancholy that overlaid a cynical sense of humor, he was holding a rectangle of cardboard and a hammer. He fished tacks from his jacket pocket and nailed the sign to the wall beside the front door.

"What does it say?" Marie Castle asked in a loud whisper.

Mr. Margolius stepped aside, as if he were obeying stage directions, to let his audience see the sign. "WARN-ING" was printed across the top in big letters that looked like old wooden handbill type.

Despair had crept into David's voice. "I think we can go in now."

The others followed him onto the porch.

Gilly said, "Good morning, Mr. Margolius. How is it in there?"

He shook his head. "I've been inspecting houses for twenty years in all parts of town, and I thought I'd seen everything—" His mournful voice trailed off, leaving an uncomfortable silence.

You had to give Gilly credit for trying, thought Dinah. She stepped up to the sign and began reading aloud:

> "WARNING: This building has been inspected and conditions found which are in violation of the Atlanta Housing Code.
>
> "It shall be unlawful for this property to be leased or occupied until requirements of the code have been met in a satisfactory manner."

"Does that mean condemned?" asked Marie.

David looked annoyed. "Yes, but we knew that."

To Margolius, he said, "Thank you for getting here so promptly. Will the houses be boarded up?"

"No," Margolius told him. And then wittingly or unwittingly, helped David's case slightly by adding, "That's just for places that are structurally unsound—the ones that have been burned or are about to fall down. They've knocked holes in the plaster and broken most of the windows, and torn off a lot of molding and baseboards. But these are well-built houses. No danger of anything falling on anybody."

David opened the front door onto a decor that Dinah had come to think of as Twentieth-century Charnel House.

Sterling seemed to have been struck speechless. His silence brought forth a spate of nervous chatter from the others as they filed in and huddled together in the only clear space, directly inside the door.

The police search of last night had rendered the place even less attractive. Clothes which had been flung together in loose piles were now scattered over the floor and mattresses.

"I wonder if it might be possible to combine these two houses into a condominium," Gilly suggested in a tone which, for her, was strangely diffident.

Ralph Swinton seized on it as if it were the architectural idea of the decade.

"Great idea," he exclaimed, and then with a wary glance at Sterling, toned it down with, "Certainly interesting."

He'd probably known Sterling long enough not to try to cram an idea down his throat but to let him think it was his own.

Gilly caught on. "It would be difficult, though, to change these ugly ducklings into swans."

Then Dinah saw on Sterling's face the look she'd seen on the faces of Ted and Amanda's customers asking the price of something they imagined to be valuable—avidity overlaid with a mask of indifference.

"Yes, it could be interesting if it's not too expensive. I'll have to get a report from you first, Ralph."

"Of course, but you know your own ideas about such things are pretty shrewd."

Dinah blushed with vicarious shame at Ralph's sycophancy and fastened her gaze on the opposite wall to keep from looking at him. There she found herself staring at something wildly incongruous: a wall phone in avocado green—one of the telephone company's new decorator colors. It hung on the wall behind a scarred and battered bar, which was a cheap imitation of the expensive models seen in the suburban excrescence called a "play room" or "family room."

She wandered over behind the bar to look at the phone numbers scrawled around the telephone on the once-white wall. Some had cryptic combinations of initials in front of them and others were simply numbers with no hint of who they belonged to. All were written in ink.

This wall also had a heavy concentration of obscenities in the omnipresent black paint.

Dinah drew in her breath and expelled it in a faint gasp. A streak of black paint had been daubed just below the cluster of phone numbers. Bright sunlight streaming through uncurtained windows showed unmistakable freshness. She glanced covertly at the others before she touched it with a forefinger. Not quite dry.

She was sure Mark Latham wouldn't have missed an obvious clue like this, but she decided to call him as soon as she could.

She tried to look like an aimless wanderer making her way to the kitchen, which mercifully appeared to have been used for storage rather than cooking. The Desperadoes were patrons of short-order drive-ins. A big green plastic trash can overflowed with cartons, wrappers, and paper cups which had contained hamburgers, french fries, soft drinks, and fried chicken, intermingled with a couple of dozen beer cans.

Beside the trash can were the things which in a more orderly household would have been kept in a tool shed, basement, or pantry. Wrenches, hammers, oily rags, and paint brushes and cans. She glanced again over her shoulder as she bent down.

One of the cans had been recently—very recently—opened and shut again, with a thin line of glistening black paint oozing from the edges around the top. She touched it gingerly to make sure and stood up to open her handbag to get out a tissue and wipe the small smudge off her finger.

She looked down and saw a smear of dirt on her beige slacks. Not a very wise choice of colors for a tour of bikers' homes. Someone else, she had noticed, had a streak of dirt or something on gray slacks.

Someone was walking toward the kitchen. She kept her hand in the handbag to wipe off the paint, then pulled out her cigarettes.

It was only Clifford. But why "only Clifford"? Why was she relieved that it wasn't one of the others? Did she suspect David or Marie Castle or Sterling or Gilly?

Suddenly she knew that she did. The reason had flitted, mothlike, through her mind while she was making her undercover investigation of the paint. And now it was gone.

Clifford held his lighter to her cigarette. "I've always heard that women head for the kitchen to check on the housekeeping, but this is surely an exception."

He looked at her closely, and lowered his voice. "What

is it, Dinah? You know you can tell your intended anything that's weighing on your heart."

"Not my heart, my mind," she said crossly. "And, dammit, now I can't remember. You scared me when you came in the door—"

He was indignant. "Scared you? Scared of your intended?"

"Clifford, will you for God's sake stop calling yourself my intended. I mean I was scared because I had my back turned and didn't know who you were when you started walking toward the door."

"You're trying to tell me in your simplistic and muddled way that you're scared of somebody in there and you don't know why?"

"I'm not too crazy about the way you put it, but that's what I mean. We'll talk about it later."

"Damn right we will. We'll probe your unconscious—shake it about like a dust mop and see what falls out."

Dinah smiled and shook her head. "Clifford, you're absolutely hopeless. But that's one of the endearing things about you to me."

"Are there others?"

"Many others. I'll write you a list."

She grinned up at him. "No, on second thought, maybe I'd better not put quite all of it in writing."

He bent his head. "Pornographic? Then whisper it."

Gilly appeared in the doorway. "This is no place for cuddling. They've gone over to the other house. Are you going?"

Clifford sighed. "I imagine it's pretty redundant. There must be a limit to the variations on this sort of household."

"They're going to check the yards between to get what they called the overall view, with the idea of making a courtyard between the two houses and adding more units at the back so both these structures can be saved and no major changes made on what's here."

"You're kidding," said Dinah. "They couldn't be talking like that about these houses."

"Oh, they're restraining themselves, throwing in bits about the terrific expense for the benefit of David and the Castle woman. But Sterling is really interested."

"Then I think we've done our duty to David," said Dinah, "and are entitled to silently steal away and take Aunt Charlotte to the shop."

"I can't see that our presence has done much good," said Clifford. "We just stood around looking embarrassed. I don't mean you, Gilly. You've played him like a skillful angler."

Gilly shrugged but looked pleased. "Well, I live on this street. I have enough material for my chapter on the Desperadoes. So I'm willing to let them go."

Clifford said, "When you finish your research on pollution, you want it to stop."

"Exactly," said Gilly, unabashed. "But he may not be hooked yet. I'd better join the others in the east wing."

She drew herself up and assumed a lady-of-the-manor air. "Before you go, though, I'd like you to polish the silver and count it and put it away."

Clifford bowed. "Yes, Madame, as soon as we finish the glassware."

"Clifford," Dinah whispered when Gilly had gone, "I found an important clue."

Clifford was impressed with the paint smear among the telephone numbers and the paint can in the kitchen. More rummaging in the heap of tools and paint buckets produced a half-dried paint brush wrapped in one of the oily rags.

"I can't help feeling that Mark Latham must have found this, too, and left it undisturbed," said Clifford.

"But why?"

"I thought maybe he wanted one of the people here this morning to feel secure about it. And maybe the police can get the paint off and read the phone number."

"Still, we better call him. I hate to go off and leave it here."

"I'll see if that phone is still connected," she told him.

It was. And she had the incredible luck of finding Mark in his office.

"No, I didn't notice it," he admitted ruefully.

"Well, you were here at night," she told him magnanimously. "I wouldn't have noticed it if the sun hadn't been shining on that smear of paint."

"I think it might be well to leave it there for a while," he said. "Watch for him in case he remembers and comes back for the paint bucket. I'll send somebody over there."

"But they're all next door now."

"Who?"

"David Winthrop and Marie Castle and Martin Sterling and his architect. Oh, and Gilly."

"Hmmm," said Mark. "In that case, my man had better park on Mimosa Way and go through the alley. Thanks a lot, Dinah. We could use you on the force."

"I'll remember that when Miles fires me."

She hung up and turned to Clifford. "He's sending somebody to watch this house in case he remembers and comes back for the paint bucket and brush."

"I think he's figuring on taking a chance on it. After all, it'll be dry probably by late this afternoon."

She grasped his arm. "Clifford! We forgot about Aunt Charlotte. What time is it?"

He looked at his watch. "Quarter to twelve. And Aunt Charlotte believes that promptness is next to cleanliness, and you know what cleanliness is next to."

Chapter Sixteen

Aunt Charlotte was sitting bolt upright in the porch swing, exuding censure as they hurried up the steps.

"Slightly delayed," Clifford told her breathlessly.

She rose majestically. "I have often told you what I think of tardiness, Clifford. I won't repeat it."

"I'm sure it will bear repeating, though, Auntie. It's borne it pretty well through the years."

He took her arm. "Shall we go in the car?"

"It's four blocks," Dinah told him. "They close up and go to lunch at twelve-thirty, but I'm sure they'll wait for us."

"Leaving no one to mind the store?" asked Aunt Charlotte. "How odd."

"They leave a sign on the door saying 'Out to lunch. Back in thirty minutes.'"

"I have seen those signs," said Aunt Charlotte. "And very exasperating they are, too. Since they don't say when you left, how can people know how much of the thirty minutes has elapsed?"

"I expect the purpose of it is to give them a more flexible lunch break," said Clifford.

Dinah sat beside Clifford in the powder-blue Cadillac,

more stiffly than she realized for he said, "Automobile snobbery takes different forms, doesn't it?"

"There is the Bentley-Rolls-Jaguar snob," he went on chattily. "He can be seen sitting on park benches smoking a pipe and reading a slender volume of verse. Dead is the only way he'd be caught in a new Cadillac. It would have to be a hearse carrying him to the cemetery.

"And the small foreign car snob. He is saying that he is a bit austere, above the scramble for acquisition of flashy possessions. But the car's a sop to his conscience because he spends a lot of money on other things, like trips to Europe.

"And there are the people like you: the old car snobs. Not a classic—just plain old. You're a variation of the small foreign car guy. Except you're saying, 'People who feel secure in their identity don't need new cars to bolster their egos.'

"But," he continued, "like the Volkswagen set, you have other status symbols. Like old worn out oriental rugs. Right?"

Her voice took on a decided chill. "You left out the new Cadillac snob, Clifford. Turn right here and left at the next corner."

"You are thinking, 'How could I have fallen for this insufferable stuffed shirt driving this big tacky car?'"

"Clifford, you seem to spend a lot of time figuring out what I'm thinking. I suppose I should be flattered."

As a matter of fact, she had been thinking exactly that, and the accuracy of what he said made it even more irritating.

"You are making assumptions without knowing the facts," he said.

Aunt Charlotte spoke up from the back seat. "Clifford,

we must have the oil checked in my car before you drive around much more."

He grinned at Dinah, his triumph so complete there was no need for words.

"Stop here," she told him.

"Here" was a Victorian relic last painted shortly before World War II. Pre-war paint was good and made to last, though, and bits of it clung stubbornly and scabrously to walls and columns and strips of gingerbread.

Towering masses of objects, mostly metal, filled the front porch and hid the front wall and windows. A pathway had been kept clear from the top of the steps to the door, but the overhang looked dangerous. Iron beds perched atop piles of trunks, benches, filing cabinets, tables, and chairs. A broken flower pot lying in the pathway appeared to have fallen off a sort of scaffolding of mantels, doors, and columns.

Clifford, parking, said, "My, they have a lot of stuff."

Getting out and standing near the car as if she were reluctant to leave it, Aunt Charlotte said, "Is it safe?"

"I was about to say 'safe as houses,' but that term doesn't seem to apply around here," said Clifford.

"It looks interesting," Aunt Charlotte declared stoutly.

"Oh, it is," Dinah told her. "Wait till you see the inside."

"If you're lucky enough to get that far," said Clifford.

A couple of well-dressed elderly matrons with ample figures and mauve hair parked behind them.

"Why don't we wait here and see if they make it?" Clifford suggested.

He took Aunt Charlotte's arm and put his other arm around Dinah's shoulder. "Come on. If the going gets rough, we can tie ourselves together with ropes."

The two women walked a few feet ahead of them, chattering and proceeding up the steps with the heedless confidence of familiarity, ignoring the stacks of loosely arranged large and lethal objects piled up six- and seven-feet high on either side of the narrow path.

One of them stopped a couple of feet from the door. "Oh, look, Edith. Right through there. That little iron table. At least I think it's iron. Just what I've been looking for to put on the terrace."

Watching them disappear through the door, Clifford said, "Who extricates this merchandise from the rubble?"

"Tim Dobson and one or two of the other winos are usually around. The ladies give them a nice tip for loading things into their cars."

"But he was knocked out and taken to the hospital last night," said Clifford. "What happens if there are no winos around? Would they be likely to ask any able-bodied man who happened to be here to get something out of there?"

"I'm afraid they would," she admitted.

Clifford fell silent and, at the top of the steps, looked up apprehensively at the ramparts of junk on either side.

"I have this uneasy feeling that it's parted temporarily, like the Red Sea, and it's going to go back together on somebody."

Behind them, Aunt Charlotte stopped. "Clifford, there's an iron bench like the one in my yard. Right through there—under that stack of iron beds and things."

"Keep moving, Auntie, or you'll be turned into a pillar of wrought iron."

"Clifford," said Dinah, "what has brought on all this biblical babbling?"

"Fear. An atavistic thing that takes me back to Aunt Charlotte's Sunday school class, which I was required to attend for three years. Fear of being buried alive, or dead, trying to get something out of there."

"Clifford, I want that bench," Aunt Charlotte announced imperiously.

He turned with his hand on the screen door. "Try to use a little self-restraint. How would you get it home? It won't fit in the trunk, we'd have to take out the seat to get it in the back. Which would you rather have, that bench or the back seat of your new car? Not to mention the rear axle."

"You're trying to make it sound impossible because you don't want to bother with it. I'm sure we can find a way."

"Not we, *you*. I've already given up on it because I tend to give up quickly on projects like that."

He opened the door and said softly, "My God!"

"The house was pretty grand in its day," said Dinah, stepping inside with the proprietary air of a tour guide.

They were standing in a tile-floored foyer, crammed with umbrella stands, hall trees, boxes, and trunks. Like the porch, it was a preview of the interior, partially visible through one of the many archways hung with stalactitic spool-and-spindle carvings.

Beyond was a large, more or less octagonal room, opening through archways into other rooms, and at the back into a hallway with a staircase ascending to a landing adorned with a stained glass window of cathedral proportions.

Seeing the place through the eyes of visitors, Dinah thought it looked as if the contents of several antique and junk shops had been dumped here by a crew of drunken workmen. She hadn't realized until now the total lack of selectivity in Ted and Amanda's shopping forays.

There were a dozen or so tables piled high with boxes of jewelry, quilts, old dolls, afghans, bedspreads, and largely unmatching china and glassware. Boxes full of miscellanea cluttered most of the floor space not occupied by a bewildering variety of furniture.

There were no counters or shelves or display cases. A many-tiered and many-mirrored overmantel was full of clocks, vases, lamps, old bottles, and several gaudy examples of Roseville pottery. In the center of the mantel stood a plaster bust of some Edwardian gentleman, possibly King Edward himself, his face partially obscured by a pink ostrich-feather boa wrapped several times around the bust and trailing over the edge of the mantel.

Under one of the archways near the mantel Amanda stood talking to the mauve-haired ladies. She saw them and waved and went on talking.

Dinah looked up to see Ted descending the stairway with George Merriman, a wealthy collector of almost everything—with large collections of almost everything except locomotive engines. He had only one of those.

He was a heavy-set man of about sixty, wearing old sneakers, old slacks and old shirt. Antique dealers who didn't know him probably locked up the jewelry case when they saw him at the door. Those who did know him, however, gave him the flattering attention due to a man who is likely to buy anything at any time.

Ted was giving him this sort of attention now. As he and Mr. Merriman reached the foot of the stairs, he acknowledged their presence with a preoccupied smile in their direction.

"We haven't had any church bells in over a year," Ted was saying regretfully as they passed by on their way to the front door. "I'll certainly be on the lookout, though."

When he had closed the door on Mr. Merriman, he picked his way toward them, smiling and shaking his head.

"Good morning, Ted," said Aunt Charlotte. "I find your place overwhelming. I hardly know where to start."

"Why don't we start with coffee in the kitchen?" said Ted.

"Mr. Merriman didn't buy anything today?" asked Dinah.

"Lord love you, child, Mr. Merriman empty-handed doesn't mean that he hasn't bought anything. It just means he hasn't bought anything that can be hauled off in anything smaller than a moving van.

"He's on the trail of church bells," Ted continued. "But the beauty of having several hundred collections is that you can always find something. He bought the enameled fieldstone facade of the old Cotton National Bank Building. It's a shame it was torn down."

"It must weigh several tons," said Dinah.

"Oh, yes, about eighty very large stones."

He glanced inquiringly at Amanda, still talking to the ladies. She gave him a vague smile.

"What is he going to do with it?" asked Clifford.

"Do with it? Mr. Merriman doesn't do anything with things. He just has them. All over his house and five-acre lot and several big storage buildings. What worries his children is what they're going to do with them when he dies. It would probably take a full day to auction off the paintings alone."

He went ahead of them through the archway, cautioning them to "watch that wardrobe door," and led them into the kitchen.

It was a vast room, apparently constructed for maximum inconvenience. Some of its labor-making devices remained: an ancient gas stove, a domed refrigerator, an old-fashioned porcelain sink, all widely separated by endless expanses of murky linoleum. It, too, was full of furniture, cardboard boxes, wooden crates, glassware, silver serving dishes and trays, and more china.

"Where do you get all this stuff?" asked Clifford.

"Oh, here and there." He was getting down an old blue-and-white enamel coffee pot. "We go to auctions and junk shops and estate sales."

He filled the pot at the sink and walked across the room to set it on the stove. "Every now and then we think of cleaning up the place, getting some shelves and display cases and arranging things neatly. But I'm afraid it would hurt our business."

"How?" asked Aunt Charlotte.

"It would spoil the fun of finding things. People appreciate things so much more when they have to work for them. They always think they're going to find a real treasure somewhere in this mess."

"I found one," said Aunt Charlotte. "An iron bench like the one in my yard."

"And talk about buried treasure," said Clifford sourly. "It's under a bunch of iron beds and metal chairs and tables. I told Aunt Charlotte we can't get it in the car."

"We might find somebody going your way in a truck," Ted suggested.

"You see, Clifford, you can always find a way to get something if you want it badly enough."

"I probably didn't want it badly enough," Clifford admitted.

"How much is it?" she asked Ted.

"I'll have to see which one it is. We'll make you a good price. Everything here is a bargain."

"Let's sit down," said Dinah.

"Where?" asked Clifford.

"Right over there."

"Right over there" was a Brontosaurus-footed round dining table surrounded by high-backed turn-of-the-century kitchen chairs, with narrow sharply carved spindles topped by a solid crosspiece.

Pulling out one for Dinah, Clifford said, "I remember these chairs, Aunt Charlotte. From Aunt Petty's kitchen. These little sharp spindles encourage erect posture. If you lean back on them, they slash into your spine."

Aunt Charlotte was roaming about, peering into crates and boxes.

"I wonder what's keeping Amanda," said Dinah.

Ted was getting cups from a glass-doored cabinet. "Those women are probably still looking."

"One of them seemed excited about an iron table on the porch," Dinah told him.

"I expect Amanda is trying to discourage them from getting it today. Tim is out back with Bill, that frail-looking friend of his. He was knocked unconscious last night, you know. Amanda said you were there. Anyway, we don't want him lifting heavy things today."

"When did they let him out of the hospital?" asked Dinah.

"Early this morning. Those old winos seem indestructible. Certainly their insides must be, to withstand the daily assault of Polly Peachtree hair tonic."

"He seemed sober last night," Clifford remarked.

"Yes, he does have those spells every now and then," said Ted. "He's still sober today."

Amanda hurried in, looking harassed. "I'm so sorry but the man has come for those chairs."

"What chairs?" asked Dinah.

"The ones you're sitting on."

Clifford said, "You mean somebody bought them?"

"Friday," said Amanda. "A young man. Young people seem to like that period—possibly because it's old enough to seem antique to them but not old enough to be expensive."

A large, long-haired young man in jeans and T-shirt appeared in the doorway. Amanda introduced him as Mr. Simms.

"I don't want to take them out from under you," he said. "I can wait or come back later."

"Oh, no," said Amanda. "No problem. If you'll just help us get more chairs from the storage room."

Clifford offered to help. Ted brought coffee to the table. Aunt Charlotte, rummaging in a crate, came up for air looking confused and glassy-eyed.

She strode over to the table. "Ted, isn't that tray Georgian silver?"

"Our specialty is decadent grandeur," he declared. "Unfortunately, I can't ask you to sit down yet, Charlotte. Somebody's here to pick up these chairs. But there are plenty more."

Intermittent thudding and crashing from the storage room indicated that other chairs were being found. Amanda and Clifford and Mr. Simms emerged, each carrying a Regency side chair upholstered in a mouldy green fuzz that looked like a thick growth of lichen.

Ted said, "I'll get the others. Might as well have the whole set out where people can see them. Although I hope nobody buys them until we—"

One of the mauve-haired ladies rushed into the room. "I'm looking for Mrs.—oh, there you are. I called home to ask my yard man to stay until I get there. He can come back and get the table."

Amanda set down the Regency chair. The woman gasped, then remembering that too-intense interest sometimes inflates prices, became elaborately offhand.

"Oh, what a sweet little chair. Do you have more of them?"

"A set of five."

"Five. A peculiar number. How much are they?"

"Sixty dollars apiece."

"Oh, dear, that seems high. I'll have to think it over."

When she had gone, Ted said, "I don't suppose there's any point in sitting down. She'll be back in a few minutes haggling over the price, which is very reasonable, and she knows it."

"I thought your policy was whetting desire through inaccessibility," said Dinah. "If so, it will be better for us to be sitting in them."

"You're right, my dear," said Ted. "Things in use are far more interesting than the ones on display. If we have an old desk that isn't moving, all we have to do is put our papers and records in it and appear reluctant to let it go.

"The thing that sends them into a frenzy, though, is a 'sold' sign. Once you put a sold sign on something, the next eight people become passionately dedicated to acquiring this rarity, and leave their phone numbers in case the buyer changes his mind."

Mr. Simms, who had been standing by diffidently, said, "May I get my chairs?"

"Yes, of course," said Ted. "Let me get someone to help you."

He went to the back door and called Tim. Tim's friend Bill came to the door with the news that Tim had gone off somewhere.

"Not feeling faint from that blow on the head, I hope," said Ted.

"Naw, sir. He'd have said something."

"Then you can help Mr. Simms with his chairs."

Bill hurried in, undismayed by the customer's look of impecunity. He was a thin, gaunt-faced old drunk, blessed with a childlike sweetness, an almost inhuman absence of greed. His needs were simple: a little money for his share of the food and rent and his daily ration of Polly Peachtree. He liked to help people, and the size of the reward seemed unimportant. In a more primitive and less avaricious society, he might have been revered as a holy man.

The two staggered out, festooned with chairs.

"Why don't we have lunch here?" said Amanda. "Dinah, you and Clifford can go get sandwiches."

Chapter Seventeen

In the car, Clifford said, "Now about your unconscious. We were planning to dig into it, remember?"

"You make my unconscious sound like an Etruscan tomb. I'm not at all sure I want it dug into."

"Oh, come now, what better thing do you have to do? All right. You were afraid of somebody there. Gilly, Sterling, Marie Castle, or David Winthrop. Why?"

Dinah said, "Turn right here and left at the next light. I don't know. I think it had something to do with the paint. And there was something else, too."

"The paint and something else," said Clifford, seemingly undaunted by this welter of vagueness.

"I remember thinking that something wasn't quite what it seemed to be. Or somebody. Or two people."

He seized on this last. "Two people. A relationship? One that isn't what it seems?"

"I think so."

"Gilly and Martin Sterling?"

"Maybe. But I don't know what."

"If they had known each other before, why would they pretend to be meeting for the first time yesterday?"

"I can't imagine. Neither of them is married. So if they

are lovers or ex-lovers, why try to hide it? Gilly certainly wouldn't care."

"When did you have this elusive thought?"

"When I was getting up from looking at that paint can. I heard somebody coming to the door. I was afraid because of something that flashed through my mind. Then I was so relieved when I saw it was you—"

"I hope you'll always feel that way about me," he said, patting her hand. "But can't you be a little more specific, Dinah?"

She shook her head. "No, I've been trying. And anyway, who can say that my unconscious is so oracular? I think we've let psychiatrists con us into thinking the unconscious is full of wisdom. Sometimes it comes up with some pretty sharp stuff, and sometimes it's just horsing around being silly."

"Also," said Clifford, "I think it performs better when it's not being monitored. So maybe if we let your unconscious rest for a while—"

"Here we are, anyway."

Clifford pulled into a small shopping center with a delicatessen. And for the next few minutes they were occupied with selecting ham, cheese, turkey, rye, and wheat bread.

Back at the shop, when they were seated around the table, Amanda said, "Charlotte has just told us the purpose of her visit. She came down to talk to me about the bobbin."

"I feel that two wrongs do not make a right," Aunt Charlotte began axiomatically.

"No, they just make two wrongs," said Clifford.

She gave him a look that said she didn't need any help from him. "I want to turn over Amanda's rightful share to her. Both our husbands made stupid wills, and I should have done it a long time ago."

"So you see," said Ted, "this little picnic is a sort of celebration."

Ted loved celebrations, thought Dinah. They were excuses for opening a bottle of something. But since there were no bottles on the premises, he made more instant coffee.

After lunch, Amanda said, "Dinah, I hope you and Clifford are feeling mellowed after this splendid picnic."

"Why?" asked Dinah suspiciously.

"Ted and I want to ask a favor of you. We were wondering if you could keep the shop this afternoon while we go to an estate sale?"

Dinah said, "I can't speak for Clifford. He doesn't seem too sanguine about tackling that junk pile on the porch."

"Not at all," said Clifford manfully. "I was only joking."

"But why should he?" asked Amanda. "We're not asking you to clean up the place. We've never done it, and we certainly wouldn't expect anyone else to."

"I'm not talking about cleaning up. You know perfectly well if you take Bill off—with Tim incapacitated and missing—that leaves Clifford to wrestle with that junk."

"But you don't have to get anything out of there," said Ted. "Just tell them you don't know the prices of any of those things on the porch. And it's the simple truth. We don't know the prices ourselves until we see the customers."

"Doesn't that apply to all this other stuff, too?" asked Dinah.

"You know our code," said Amanda. "Most of the things have the code price, and you can always come down a little."

"For what reason?" asked Dinah. "That you're running a special on feather boas or busts of Edward VII?"

"You don't need any excuse to come down on the price," Amanda told her.

"This lesson in sales psychology is intimidating me," said Clifford. "I think I'll let Dinah handle sales, and I'll carry stuff to the cars."

Aunt Charlotte, looking heavy-eyed, said, "Clifford, I must ask you to take me back to the house. I feel the need of a little nap."

"All right, Auntie. And we'll stop by a filling station and have the oil checked and buy some gas."

After they had gone, Dinah heated water for more coffee, poured it into one of the chipped cups, and drifted out to the living room.

In a cluttered corner, she found a 1920 reproduction of a Jacobean chair and a World War I helmet to use for an ash tray.

The sudden solitude was at first disquieting, then restful. Perhaps in the vast quietude of the old house she could bring back the elusive thought.

But the silence was not absolute. Cars and trucks whooshed by on Ponce de Leon a block away. A power mower whined and sputtered down the street. A dog was barking in an annoying pattern of alternating silence and frenzied yapping. During the stillness, she found herself listening for the next seizure of barking.

Closer noises intruded. The old house whispered and muttered to itself. Acorns fell on the roof and rolled down to lodge in the gutters or fall to the ground. Now, along with the dog's bark, she was listening for the next one to crack on the shingles and tumble down the steep roof.

What was the matter with her, anyway? It must be the

cumulative effect of the whole weekend, starting with Aunt Charlotte's telegram. She looked back to the pre-telegram serenity and marveled.

Saturday morning she'd have been reluctant to pay a fortune teller who might have had the prescience to predict this crazy weekend—that she would discover that one of Aunt Charlotte's banker nephews was what she'd always wanted; that Aunt Charlotte was an old acquaintance of the leader of the Desperadoes; that her talk with him had probably precipitated his murder.

He must have been desperately afraid, sauntering down the street, keeping up his facade of the big bad biker. And seeing, of all people, his old Sunday school teacher.

The only warning of another presence was a faint clicking, like someone brushing against one of the stacks of china in the kitchen.

As she drew in her breath, her mind busied itself with all the sensible arguments against panic. It could be a mouse. Ted and Amanda kept traps all over the place. It could be her imagination.

But another part of her brain impelled her to reach in her handbag and grope for the weapon that most women carry. Her fingers closed around a small cylinder, rejected it as too small, closed around another, and pulled it out. Hair spray.

This was just in case. She wasn't hanging around for a confrontation. She was heading for the front door. Fast. She stood up and reluctantly but compulsively turned her head just far enough to see the archway into the back hall.

And there he was. With all the trappings of hallucination. She had been thinking about the biker, and her mind had conjured him up. But this wasn't Artie Stockton, materializing as too-solid ectoplasm.

This was Tim's biker. His face distorted by a black-stocking mask. His hair covered by a biker's black cap, an imitation of a Civil War soldier's cap. Bikers don't wear gray slacks and black loafers.

She turned and started running, weaving and dodging obstacles between her and the door. Her hand swept something off one of the tables. It crashed and broke. She heard him gasp close behind her. He, too, was finding it rough going.

She'd make it rougher. She knocked off something else as she ran past a table. Something large. It fell with a metallic clang, directly in his path. He said something under his breath. She caught a brief glimpse of the next thing she knocked off—a brass umbrella stand.

She reached the foyer. At the door, she grasped the knob, turning and pulling. The door was either stuck or locked.

His breathing was harsh, filling the small space with the grotesquely amplified rasping of a man in an iron lung she'd seen when she was a child.

She whirled around to face him. Her finger pressed the button, aimed it at his eyes.

His hands reached for her. One grasped her throat, the other her arm holding the spray.

He was forcing her arm down. And then the pressure was suddenly released on her throat and arm. She almost fell forward. His arms were crossed over his face, protecting his eyes and nose and mouth. He turned, blinded and choking to stumble through the archway.

She watched his staggering retreat through the big room. He blundered into a table full of vases and china, then backed off from it. His vision must be clearing because he was running now, still gasping and choking.

She watched him with the primitive exultation of one who has triumphed in a death struggle.

As he ran through the archway, she saw just above the cuff of his gray slacks the smear of paint she had seen this morning.

Out of sight in the kitchen, he gave a grunt as if he had run into something else.

Foolishly, she ran after him, not giving a thought to the danger of his returning vision. She stopped in the kitchen doorway, leaned weakly against the door.

He was lying on the floor. Clifford knelt beside him. He looked up at her. "The front door was locked. He put the out-to-lunch sign on it. I figured something funny was going on."

He looked again at the unconscious man. "Better get something to tie him up with."

Chapter Eighteen

Three hours later, Dinah was sitting beside Clifford at the table where they had sat at the Saturday night meeting of the Pseudo-Intellectual Society of the South.

The only other member present, however, was Gilly. The others at the table were Mark Latham, Ted and Amanda, and Martin Sterling.

Mark said, "When did you know who he was, Dinah?"

"It all sort of clicked together, like one of those interlocking puzzles, when I saw the paint smear on the side of his pants' cuff, where other people could see it but he couldn't."

Mark took a sip of his coffee and set the mug down on the red plastic top. "We've got somebody working on that paint now, taking it off the wall. I'm sure it will be his phone number under there."

"Do you think you'll be able to read it?" asked Amanda.

"Pretty sure. Those numbers are in ink on a plaster wall. We think the numbers will be scratched into the plaster."

"Has he said anything yet?" This was from Ted, whose round face looked drawn and haggard.

"No, he hasn't admitted anything. He says he won't talk to anybody except his lawyer."

"Theron Caldwell," muttered Ted, staring into his glass. He looked up at Mark. "You don't have any proof."

"Oh, we're getting it," Mark said easily. He smiled at Dinah. "Not the kind of evidence that Dinah collected. It made her realize who he was, but only just before Clifford clipped him in the kitchen. It's more like ESP, and not admissible in court."

"How did you know, Dinah?" asked Gilly.

"When I saw the paint smear on his pants after I doused him with hair spray, I remembered the other things. Like— well, when he came to our house for lunch yesterday, he claimed he had slept late and hadn't heard about the murder until he got up and out of the house.

"But in the kitchen," she went on, "where you were mixing drinks, Ted, you said you'd called him early Sunday morning to tell him about the murder."

Gilly said, "Liars should have extraordinarily good memories."

"Yes," said Clifford. "Several times he pretended ignorance, and later let it slip out that he knew things. He said a couple of times he hadn't seen the inside of those houses, said that he and Marie Castle had come over there last night to see what kind of shape they were in. But at Gilly's a little later he was worried about whether he should have them cleaned up and said something about the clothes strewn around and the obscenities on the walls.

"Of course," he continued, "somebody could have told him about it. But who? Dinah didn't tell him on the phone. I was standing beside her while she talked to him. He asked how they looked inside and she said 'bad' or 'awful.' He and Marie Castle were claiming that she hadn't seen the inside of them, either. Gilly didn't tell him after we went to her apartment. Everybody talked about how bad they looked, but nobody went into detail about it while he was around."

"There was another little discrepancy yesterday afternoon," said Dinah. "Remember when we were talking about the bikers' houses, and he said he knew the owner?"

"I remember it," said Martin Sterling.

"But on the phone last night, when he called to make sure I was going over there this morning, he said he didn't know her, had never met her.

"He said he was going out to the owner's house to get the keys from her, but she was there with him, wherever he was, listening on an extension."

Mark stared at her. "Ah, I haven't heard this. Did she say something?"

"No, I heard her bracelets clinking. Those two bracelets with dangling coins and charms. I asked David what that clinking noise was and he said he was tapping his pen on the phone, that he always did it when he was nervous. Then later, at Gilly's, they were clinking when she moved her arm and I recognized it, but only subconsciously, I suppose."

"Very observant, my child," Mark told her approvingly.

She glared at him, and he grinned. "I'm not making light of your deductions. I really mean it."

He shook his head ruefully. "I'm in no position to sneer at your detective work. I missed that wet paint."

Clifford said, "Dinah saw the paint smear on his slacks sometime while we were outside or after we went in the house—"

"And I forgot it," she said. "In the kitchen, right after I found the paint bucket, I looked down and saw a smudge of dirt on my slacks and remembered seeing a smear of something on somebody's gray slacks, but I thought it was dirt. And everybody there was wearing gray slacks except me. Gilly and Clifford and David and Marie Castle. And you and Ralph Swinton, Mr. Sterling."

Sterling laughed. "So we were. And mine were pretty dirty when I got back to my room."

"But the paint smear was near the cuff of his slacks," said Dinah. "The paint on the wall was too high up for him to have got it from brushing against it. He got it on them the night before when he was fooling around in the dark with the bucket of paint.

"The rest of it is even vaguer," she continued. "I thought that David was strangely indifferent to Mrs. Castle's looks when he was sitting beside her at Gilly's. I figured it was nervousness over selling you those houses, Mr. Sterling. It meant a lot to him. You might buy others if you bought those.

"Then the idea just sort of accumulated that it was the indifference of familiarity. I'm not explaining this very well," she said haltingly. "She called him David this morning. Which doesn't really mean anything. It was the way she said it. And also she wasn't flirting with him."

Gilly pitched in loyally. "I think it's very clear. She's the type of woman who automatically flirts with men. If there's some man she's not being coquettish with, it means she's passed that stage with him. You can pick out the husband of a woman like that when you walk into a roomful of people. He's the one she's not flirting with."

"We've talked to her husband," said Mark. "He claims just the opposite of what Mrs. Castle told us. That she handled the rentals of those two houses. He said he didn't know the bikers were there until the neighbors started calling to complain about them."

He glanced uneasily at Ted, who probably was gathering ammunition for the defense. "I think Mrs. Castle will talk. We picked her up about an hour ago. She's scared and getting hysterical. I'm going to let her simmer for a while and go back and talk to her."

Clifford said, "What worries me is that I don't see how he had time to get to the bikers' house after he called Dinah last night. We left right away, as soon as she hung up the phone, and walked around the corner. And Tim Dobson was there. He'd apparently been watching the flashlight for at least a couple of minutes."

"You're assuming he called from his house," Mark told him. "I think he called from here—in the bar, which is closed on Sunday night. Custer's Last Stand faces on Mimosa Way, but the alley behind it goes past the bikers' back yard and joins the other alley where we found Stockton's body.

"Garbage trucks used to go through the alleys, but the city stopped the alley pickups several years ago. A lot of people extended their back fences to include the alleys, but those two are still open."

"You mean the one that comes out on Tarrant Place?" asked Dinah. "Then he must have left as soon as he hung up the phone, gone out the back door of the bar and down the alley to the bikers' house. And he went back the same way, after hitting Tim with the flashlight."

Mark said, "I think he was going in the back door of the bar when you were running past here, going up the block of Tarrant Place between Fern Terrace and Mimosa Way. I think he saw you and thought that you saw him."

"But I didn't. I wasn't looking at anything. I was just running, trying to get around the corner to the pay phone in front of the bar."

"I think," said Mark, "he was watching you when you

found the paint smear on the wall, and he saw you looking at the spot of paint on his slacks."

"But if I had seen him going in the back door of the bar he could have explained it later," Dinah objected.

"Not too well," Mark said, "especially if he was still wearing that black jacket he picked up in the house as an impromptu disguise. Remember, he had told you on the phone he was going to Marie Castle's house to get the keys. So what was he doing running down the alley and going in the back door of the bar?"

"He was safe as long as no one suspected him," put in Amanda. "Once the police started looking into his activities, he was lost."

Ted's voice trembled but his face remained impassive. "I—I saw him with her—the Castle woman, in a bar downtown about a year ago, shortly after his divorce from a very nice girl. I didn't know who she was. I knew it was the same woman, though, from your description of her this morning, Amanda. Silver-blonde with a lot of jewelry. When you told me she owned those houses and what the neighbors were saying, I started worrying."

He shook his head. "Actually, I started worrying about him four or five years ago, after his mother died. My brother ran off and left them when David was fifteen . . . He seemed in too much of a hurry to make money. Pulling shady deals. But nothing—nothing like this."

Mark said, "I think I know why he was forced to make contact with Artie Stockton. Mrs. Castle's husband asked her for a divorce about a year ago. She refused. He set a private detective on her trail and she caught on. He got evidence of her affair with David Winthrop, but Castle missed the big stuff by telling his private eye just to follow her around town. She went to Mexico a couple of times and the detective didn't go. Castle claims he didn't know about the drug trade, that he thought they were just ordinary business trips, and he'd save money by not having her tailed on buying trips."

"So," said Sterling, "he had to meet Artie Stockton somewhere to hand over the stuff to him and collect the proceeds. And he decided on going to the house in that disguise."

"Yes," said Mark. "He created a mystery figure by going to the front door in that disguise. He was afraid Stockton might recognize him because he'd seen him at the bar and around the neighborhood. He'd go out the back door of the bikers' house and down the alley and into the back door of the bar, shedding his disguise at the other end of the alley after he made sure he wasn't being followed. He could put all of it in his raincoat pockets—dark glasses, soft hat, and beard. We didn't find them here so they must be at his house. We're searching it now."

"How do you think Stockton found out who he was?" asked Sterling.

"Probably Stockton is the only person who knew that. But we can guess that he must have followed him once when he went out the back door. Since we don't know when that was, we don't know how far along he'd got on his blackmailing. As far as making at least one phone call, though, on account of the phone number on the wall.

"Maybe he agreed to meet Stockton in the alley to give him a pay-off. And probably took a knife from the bar."

Clifford said, "How could he get Stockton to stand still while he cut his throat? He was a powerful-looking guy."

"In the autopsy they found a lump on the back of his head, bad enough to have knocked him out. After that it was easy."

"Was he following Dinah after she left the bikers' house this morning?" asked Sterling.

Dinah said, "He knew we were taking Aunt Charlotte to see the shop."

"So," said Mark, "he must have been hanging around out back to watch for a chance when she was alone. He saw everybody else leaving."

"But customers could have come in," Sterling objected.

"He hung the out-to-lunch sign on the door and went in and locked it," said Mark. "He had the biker's disguise with him in case something went wrong. His disguises weren't elaborate. It took only a few seconds to put on either of them. He must have gone through one of those rooms opening into the living room and into the back hall. He came out when he was sure Dinah was alone."

"I still don't understand," said Sterling. "If Dinah was going to tell anybody her suspicions, she had several chances."

"I believe he thought she might be planning to blackmail him."

Dinah gasped. "Oh, he couldn't have thought I'd do such a thing."

"Why not?" said Gilly. "The dishonest attribute honesty to lack of guts. And he knew you had plenty of guts."

Mark stood up. "I've got to go see if they've found anything in his house."

The door opened and Aunt Charlotte came in, stood looking around till she saw them, and headed for their table.

She stopped beside Mark as the men stood up. "Captain Latham! I've remembered it."

Her glance at Ted held a mixture of apology and

apprehension. But with her life-long policy of duty before pleasure, she plunged on.

"It was David Winthrop. He came out of the bar here and went to his car—to get something out of the glove compartment. His car was parked directly across from us. I'm sure that's who Arthur Stockton was looking at when we met each other in front of Amanda's house Saturday night. He looked across the street and stopped talking just after he said that he knew too much and knew who . . . But he didn't finish it. And there was nobody else in sight except the people fighting next door, and he had seen all of them while we were talking."

"Thank you so much, Mrs. Prentiss," Mark said formally. "That will be a great help in our investigation."

Aunt Charlotte, looking around at the grave faces, appeared confused and puzzled as Clifford moved to her side.

"Clifford, why didn't you wake me up? I'd have slept all afternoon if those young people next door hadn't started practicing again. When I found out there was nobody home, I thought I'd find you here."

Clifford patted her arm. "You've been hanging around in bars too much, Aunt Charlotte. I'm taking you home tomorrow."

"But I'm coming back."

"Coming back? Here?"

"Yes, Clifford. Why should you have a monopoly on being tired of Andrewsville? I've been tired of it much longer than you have. I want to get an apartment here and then look for a job."

Gilly sat up and leaned forward. "Ah, now you're talking. I need somebody to help me with research."

"But she won't pay you more than the minimum wage,

Charlotte," said Amanda. "Ted and I need somebody to help in the shop."

"And I," said Sterling, "need a resident manager for my Midtown properties."

Ted's face brightened. "This calls for a drink."

Aunt Charlotte smiled and sat down. "Indeed it does."